Some Job

Some Job

JAMES PATTINSON

ROBERT HALE · LONDON

ISBN 0 7090 6274 5

Robert Hale Limited
Clerkenwell House
Clerkenwell Green
London EC1R 0HT

2 4 6 8 10 9 7 5 3 1

TALNET	
Morley Books	8.10.98
F	£16.99

Photoset in North Wales by
Derek Doyle & Associates, Mold, Flintshire.
Printed in Great Britain by
St Edmundsbury Press, Bury St Edmunds, Suffolk.
Bound by WBC Book Manufacturers Limited, Bridgend.

CONTENTS

Chapter One

ISLAND IN THE SUN

The best that could be said about the St Joseph Airport was that it served its purpose adequately. It was modest in scale: just a few white-roofed buildings and a concrete runway that would never have taken the weight of a jumbo or anything approaching it in size. But this did not matter, because you would never find any transatlantic jets dropping in there with their hundreds of passengers; it was simply not in that class and never would be. There was not the traffic.

Frank Devon had travelled from England via Miami International Airport, and the last part of the flight had been made in a rather small twin-engined machine which had accommodation for no more than thirty or so passengers. For St Joseph was not one of the big players in the tourist league, and the holiday trade, though a useful aid to the island's economy, was strictly limited. Moreover, it was not on the visiting list of any of those monstrous cruise liners that were now sailing out of Miami to flood so many of the Caribbean islands with tourists. It had been spared that intrusion, but in consequence had missed out on the revenue that might have been brought by those pleasure-seeking thousands. So it had to find other ways of making a living.

Devon himself was not going there for a holiday, though Detective Superintendent Alfred Lee had suggested rather sourly that it would in effect be something rather in this nature and that Devon was a lucky sod to be chosen for the assignment.

'Could just do with a spell of tropical sunshine meself. Palm trees, golden beaches, blue lagoons and all that nonsense. Suit me a treat. But no such luck for yours truly. I've got to stay here and mind the shop while you go gadding off on a spree like this. Tell me why that should be, lad? Just tell me why?'

'I don't know, sir. Spin of the wheel, maybe.'

'There's no justice in the world,' Lee said. 'Here am I, old enough to be your father, and when did I ever land a cushy number like this? I ask you, when?'

Devon suspected that this question was merely rhetorical and called for no answer; so he offered none.

'Well,' Lee said, 'just you behave yourself while you're there. Remember that you're the representative of a force with a reputation to maintain, and don't go doing nothing to bring it into disrepute. See what I mean?'

'Yes, sir. I see what you mean.'

'Then bear it in mind, lad, bear it in mind.'

When he said this Detective Superintendent Alfred Lee

straightened up his bony frame to its full six feet and three inches and squared his shoulders for a few moments before letting them revert to the normal rounded position which the weight of passing years had forced upon them.

'That's all then. Now get to hell out of here. I have work to do even if you haven't.'

Christine stared at him in unbelief when he broke the news to her, and he could see that she was far from pleased about it.

'You're going where?'

He repeated the information, though he was sure she had heard perfectly the first time round.

'To St Joseph. It's an island in the West Indies.'

'Why?' she demanded.

'It's an exchange between police forces. A kind of goodwill thing. I go there and they send one of their men here. Like that we each gain experience in the way our opposite numbers go about things.'

'So why you?'

'How do you mean, why me?'

'It's plain English, isn't it? Why did they pick you for the job? Must be loads of others who could have done it just as well.'

'Yes, but—'

His hesitation was all the hint she needed. 'Don't tell me. You asked for it, didn't you? You bloody well applied for it.'

'Well, not exactly. They were asking for volunteers to take the job, and I—'

'And you stepped forward and volunteered. It's like I said, you asked for it.'

'If you put it that way.'

'What other way is there of putting it? How many other volunteers were there?'

'I don't know. Quite a few. I'd say.'

'And they had to pick you.'

'Yes.'

'I wonder why,' she said. And then: 'Does your wife get to go with you to this West Indian paradise?'

'I'm afraid not.'

'Just as I might have expected. Nothing in it for me. And how long will you be away?'

'About three months.'

She sniffed, and her sniffs could be very expressive. 'Now that is nice, isn't it? That is really nice. So I'm to be left here all on my ownsome while you're away having a fine old time of it down there on your island in the sun. Great!'

'I'm not going there for a fine old time. It's a job of work like any other.'

She sniffed again. Devon had sometimes thought that no one in the world could put more meaning into a common or garden sniff than Chris.

'Some job,' she said. 'How many crimes do you expect to clear up while you're there?'

'Now you're being silly,' he said.

But he could appreciate her point of view. Perhaps she had

good reason to feel aggrieved. He had sprung this thing on her without warning, presenting it as a *fait accompli* and not giving her a chance to express an opinion on the matter, so was it any wonder that she was mad at him?

'You might at least have discussed it with me first,' she said. 'But I suppose it didn't even occur to you. I suppose my wishes don't count for anything these days. That's it, isn't it? I'm just a bloody doormat and you can walk all over me just as you please. All right then; all bloody right.'

'You don't have to make such a big issue of it,' he said. 'Maybe it's for the best really.'

She gave a questioning lift of the eyebrows. 'I think you'd better explain that, because frankly I don't see the logic. What exactly are you trying to say?'

'Oh, for God's sake, Chris, do I have to spell it out? You know as well as I do that things haven't been going right between you and me. Maybe it's my fault; maybe it's nobody's fault; maybe it's just the way of the world. I don't know. Perhaps we need to take a break, give ourselves time to reflect, work out what's gone wrong.'

He felt he was making a hash of it, and he could see that it was not going down at all well with her. She was frowning and biting her lip, and he feared she might be about to flare up and show her temper and maybe start throwing things at him, as she had done on occasion. But she did not. She just said:

'So you want to get away from me?'

'Just for a while. Just to see how it works out.'

'I'll tell you how it could work out,' she said; and there was a chill in her voice. 'It could work out with me not being here when you come back. Have you thought of that?'

'No, I haven't thought of that.'

'Then you'd better start thinking about it right now. Because it could happen, you know. It could just happen.'

He understood that she was making a threat to leave him, and he did not doubt that she was serious. It could mean the final break-up of their marriage, nothing less. And he wondered whether he would care. He gave the merest hint of a shrug and said:

'Well, Chris, it's up to you.'

They had been married for just a couple of years. He had met her in the course of his work. He had been a detective constable at the time, and he had been called to her flat to investigate a break-in. The flat was no great shakes, but she was. Her name was Christine Walker, and she was petite and black-haired, with a kind of elfin face and a pair of the most lustrous dark eyes he had ever seen. He was attracted at once, and apparently the attraction was mutual. She told him later that when he walked in she didn't give a damn about the things that had been stolen and didn't really want them back. She just wanted him.

He never got the villain who had made the break-in, but he got her, and that was all that mattered to him then. She was sharing the flat with another girl named Elsa Waite, a rather limp blonde who hardly registered at all on his consciousness; she was just a vague figure in the background.

At that time Chris had a job with a travel agency, but the agency was heading for the rocks and it hit them soon after Devon got to know her. So that job was gone and she was having difficulty landing another when he came up with the proposal that they should get married. She hardly needed to think about it for more than a second; it seemed such a good idea.

'You're sure it's what you want, Frank darling?'

'Of course I'm sure. Aren't you?'

'Oh yes,' she said. 'You bet your life I am.'

She gave up her share of the flat. Miss Waite said she would miss her, but she already had someone else lined up to take over the partnership when Miss Walker left, so it would make no difficulty for her.

The wedding was a quiet ceremony at a register office, because that was the way they both wanted it. It was their day, not just an excuse for a lot of other people to celebrate and drink too much and make idiotic speeches.

They spent the honeymoon on Capri, and it was like a heavenly dream.

'What a piece of luck,' she remarked one day as they lay basking in the sun.

'Luck?' he said. 'I don't get you.'

'But you have got me,' she said; and laughed. 'Anyway, I was thinking of that break-in. If it hadn't happened we might never have set eyes on each other.'

'I see what you mean. So we owe our happiness to a petty thief. What a turn of fate.'

'Maybe we were just born lucky.'

'I'll go along with that,' he said.

It was fine for a year; things could not have been better. Then it started to go wrong. He could not have said precisely when; it was such a gradual process. They had had the occasional argument before; it would have been a miracle if they had not. But these had been mere passing clouds, quickly forgotten. Later the clouds became darker and there were more of them. The early magic had been lost; perhaps it had been just too good to last.

The nature of his work did not help. She complained that she could never be sure when he would be home. And often he would arrive to discover that she was not there to welcome him. They had bought a rather dilapidated terraced house in the Hammersmith area on a mortgage, and it was eating up money on repairs and renovations. To help pay for all this Chris had taken jobs, but these had all been tempporary and part-time, and when she was not working she complained of boredom. She complained of a lot of things. Sometimes it seemed to him that life with her had become one long complaint.

It should never have been like that.

'There she is now,' the woman said. 'There's my island right down there like it was jus' dropped from heaven into de sea.'

The woman was sitting next to Devon on the window side.

She was black and fat and maybe getting on for forty. She had talked a lot on the flight from Miami, and by this time he knew quite a bit about her. She was no holidaymaker; she was going home after five years away. She had had a job in New York, housekeeping for a doctor and his attorney wife. They were nice people and the pay had been good, but she had been homesick. So she was going back to St Joseph, where she might be out of work and struggling to make ends meet. But she was cheerful about it; not at all apparently daunted by the prospect. For her it was home and there was no place like it.

'You on holiday?' she asked.

Devon shook his head. 'Not this time.'

'Business trip, huh?'

'You could say that.'

He did not tell her what kind of business it was, and she did not ask.

The plane was lined up with the runway and was losing height.

'Here we go,' the woman said. 'Wait for de bump.'

Devon sat back and waited for the bump.

Chapter Two

QUARTERS

'Sergeant Devon?' the man said. And it was more of a statement than a question.

He was black and his skin had a shine to it, as though it had been polished like a guardsman's toecap. He was tall and lean and his head was shaved. It looked like a cannon-ball. Devon judged him to be somewhere in his thirties.

'That's me.'

'Guessed it,' the man said. Grinning, showing teeth like pearls. 'My name's Marmaduke Morton. Detective Sergeant. Folks call me Duke. I'm to be your partner long's you're here. Show you the way around.'

Morton was wearing an immaculate biscuit-coloured tropical suit that was a perfect fit and looked as though it had just been cleaned and pressed. The jacket was unbuttoned and Devon caught a glimpse of the butt of an automatic pistol in a leather holster.

It would have taken no great powers of detection for Morton to single him out from the rest of the passengers coming from the plane; the other whites were pretty obviously tourists and the blacks could be disregarded.

Morton was offering his hand and Devon clasped it. He felt as though his own hand had been enveloped by the tentacles of a small warm octopus.

'How's that plan sound to you?' Morton asked.

'Sounds fine, Duke. And my name's Frank. People call me Frank. No title.'

Morton failed to get it straightaway. Then he gave a high-pitched giggling laugh. 'Oh man, that's good, that is. No title, huh? I guess you'd have to search long an' hard for me in that book with all the lords and ladies inside. What you call it?'

'Debrett?' Devon suggested.

'That's it. That's the one. Debrett,' Morton said, laying the emphasis on the first syllable as though naming some character named Brett with the initial 'D'.

'I got a car right outside,' he said. 'Let's go.'

He lent a hand with Devon's luggage and led the way out of the airport building to a green Rover parked outside. It was still early afternoon, with the sun shining from an almost cloudless sky and a slight breeze tempering the heat.

'Idea is this,' Morton said. 'We go first to police headquarters, introduce you to the superintendent and some of the other guys, later show you where you'll be livin'. Okay with you?'

'I'm in your hands,' Devon said.

The hands were on the steering-wheel now and the car was heading away from the airport along a road from which the sea could be seen not far away on the left, green mountains in the distance on the other side. It was quite a short drive; then they were at the outskirts of Arthurton, the only port of any size and capital of the island, which was situated on the shores of a small bay.

Devon was not favourably impressed by what he saw now; a jumble of shacks constructed of any material that had come to hand at little or no expense; corrugated iron, sacking, bits of timber maybe found as flotsam washed up on the beach, tar-paper, flattened-out oil drums; all hanging together as if by some miracle which might at any moment withdraw its power and send the entire ramshackle cluster of miserable dwellings crashing to the ground. Goats and chickens and even the odd pig foraged for sustenance in the garbage that lay around, while swarms of black children played noisily wherever there was a square yard of space to accommodate them. Men and women too were going about their business or simply idling in the sun.

Morton seemed to feel obliged to apologize for this far from salubrious introduction to Arthurton.

'Shanty town. Jus' somehow growed. Need bulldozers come in, flatten the lot. My opinion.'

'Then where would all these people live?'

Morton shrugged. 'Not my problem.'

Which was of course the easy way out. Wash your hands of it. Look the other way.

'Where do the richer people live?'

'Other side of town. That's the classy area. You'll see.'

They came to a street market, humming with life; stalls of fish, vegetables, fruit, meat, clothing, hardware, junk. Nearer the centre of the town were shops, ice-cream parlours, bars, hotels. some old houses with wrought-iron balconies and window shutters. There was a congestion of cars, buses, lorries, bicycles, pedestrians. Radios blasting out West Indian music mingled with the impatient sounding of motor horns.

Police headquarters was a fairly large white stone building with a paved forecourt on which some patrol cars and other vehicles were parked. Morton brought the Rover to a halt, and he and Devon got out and walked to some wide steps leading up to the front entrance of the place. Inside was a kind of foyer, a desk on the left, behind which was a sergeant in blue shirt and trousers. Some men and women were sitting on a bench on the right, just waiting it seemed for someone to take notice of them.

'Wait here a minute,' Morton said.

He walked over to the desk and had a word with the sergeant in the blue uniform. This other sergeant picked up a telephone and spoke into it. Then he replaced the receiver and gave a nod. Morton returned to where Devon was standing.

'Okay,' he said. 'Let's go see the big man.'

They went up a flight of stairs and along a corridor until they came to a door on which was some gold lettering that spelt out the words: Detective Superintendent Calthorpe Christy.

Morton tapped on the door with his knuckles and a voice rasped out an invitation to them to enter.

'Come.'

They went in. The superintendent was seated behind a desk on which were three telephones and a sheaf of official-looking papers. He was a large grossly fat man who had certainly not been pounding any pavements on foot-patrol for a good many years. With all that weight to carry, he would never have caught an escaping criminal by running; he would have been more likely to suffer a heart attack.

'So,' he said in that rasping voice, staring at Devon with a pair of eyes which seemed to be peering over a rampart of moist flesh, 'you are our visiting police officer.'

Devon agreed that he was.

'And what have you come to do here? Teach us how to do our job or be taught by us how to do yours?'

Devon answered guardedly: 'Neither, I think, sir. I believe it's supposed to be for experience.'

'Experience. Now that's a good word.' Christy chuckled, flesh quivering like a vast blackcurrant jelly. 'I think I can guarantee it'll be an experience. Not like London. Not at all like London, I'd say.'

'I didn't expect it would be.'

'Then you won't be disappointed. Sergeant Morton will give you the run-down on things. Take your cue from him and you won't go far wrong.'

Christy rambled on for a time, but it was evident to Devon

that he did not regard the addition to his team of a detective from England as any great deal. Finally he expressed a hope that Devon would enjoy his stay and dismissed the two sergeants with a flip of the hand.

'What you think of old C.C.?' Morton asked when they had left the big man's weighty presence.

Devon dodged the question. He said: 'Was he always as fat as that?'

Morton grinned. 'You noticed?'

'I'm trained to be observant.'

'Well,' Morton said, 'he never was thin; not as I recall. But he could carry his weight. Since he got to be superintendent seems like he's just let it rip. Maybe that's the way it takes some guys when they get to sittin' behind a desk too much.'

'Think it'll ever take you that way?'

Morton seemed to find this suggestion highly amusing. It made him laugh. 'No chance. I'm just one of nature's lean kind. Maybe I worry too much.'

Devon thought this unlikely. Morton did not impress him as being an habitual worrier.

Morton took him on a tour of the building and introduced him to some of his new colleagues, who seemed to regard him as a curiosity, a white man in an otherwise all-black community. But they were all friendly enough and none of them seemed to resent his presence.

After the tour Morton suggested that maybe it was time to show Devon where he would be living during his stay on the island.

'Hope you'll like it.'

When he saw the accommodation that had been arranged for him Devon was pleasantly surprised. It could certainly have been a lot worse. It was away out on the south side of Arthurton and they drove there in the Rover past a lot of houses that Morton told him belonged to some of the more prosperous inhabitants. These were so impressive that Devon could not help reflecting that there had to be quite a number of islanders who were making a packet, even though the economy of St Joseph was reputed to be in rather poor shape. The contrast between one side of Arthurton and the other could not have been more marked: shanty town to the north, desirable residences to the south.

The accommodation earmarked for his own use turned out to be a chalet, built for the tourist trade but apparently not in demand at that time.

'Right now,' Morton said, 'things are slack in that line, so you're in luck. You'll find this a whole lot better than the barracks.'

He explained that 'the barracks' was a dormitory block where the unmarried members of the Arthurton police force were housed. Devon was glad he had been spared that, though he was rather surprised that the authorities should have been so concerned for his comfort.

The chalet was in among some palm trees, a hundred yards or so from the sandy shore of the bay, and from that shore one could gaze across at the jetties sticking out from the Arthurton waterfront. It seemed a pleasant situation, but Morton said that the favourite holiday resort was on the other side of the island, at a place called Logan's Bay.

'This project never took off. It was supposed to be a rival to Logan's, but when they'd put up three or four of these chalets it all came to a stop. Maybe the money ran out. I d'know. Some you win, some you lose, I guess.'

Devon could see the other chalets through the trees; they were beginning to look a little dilapidated.

'No one in those?'

'Not at this moment in time. There've been squatters. We had to throw them out. I'd say the owners are glad to have a cop in this one, keep an eye on things.'

'So that's my job?'

'You don't have to break your neck over it,' Morton said. 'But if you do see anything suspicious wouldn't do no harm to pass the word.'

The interior of the chalet was fairly basic; no luxury. There were two bedrooms, a combined sitting and dining room, a small kitchen and a bathroom with no tub but a shower. Electricity and water were laid on, but there was no heating system; in that climate it was hardly necessary.

There was evidence that someone had been in to prepare the place for his occupation: one of the beds was made and some provisions had been brought in. The refrigerator was humming softly.

'Suit you?' Morton asked.

'Suits me fine. What's the drill now?'

'What I suggest is you leave your kit here, then we take a ride round, let you get the feel of things. Later we go to my place, introduce you to the wife and kids, have a meal, talk. How's that strike you?'

'Sounds great,' Devon said. 'But I don't want to put Mrs Morton to any trouble.'

Morton grinned. 'No trouble. She expectin' you. Be pretty damn upset I turn up and you not with me. She a real inquisitive woman. Any new face aroun', she jus' gotta see it.'

'Well,' Devon said, 'I'd hate to disappoint her. Though maybe it'll turn out she doesn't like the face after all.'

'Frank,' Morton said, 'face like yours any woman of taste is jus' bound to like. And Ida, she sure does got taste.'

Chapter Three

A GOOD TEAM

They drove round Arthurton, with Morton pointing out features of the town. It had been a haunt of buccaneers in the bad old days, and Devon wondered whether that past of lawlessness had echoes in modern times. Piracy might no longer be a favoured occupation, but there were plenty of more up-to-date methods of turning a dishonest penny.

'Is there much crime here?' he asked.

Morton gave a laugh. 'Know any place there ain't?'

Devon gathered that the answer was yes. He was not surprised. Even island Edens had their snakes.

They drove down to the harbour and along the waterfront. There were two small merchant ships lying alongside one of the piers, taking on cargo, and there was one at another pier discharging, but the rest of the craft in the harbour were boats of various sizes and a number of sea-going yachts with their sails furled. There were some transit sheds by the quay and a harbour-master's office with a lifebuoy hanging on one wall.

There was a stray dog giving a lamp-post a wash and a lot of idlers were loafing around or keeping an eye on those citizens who were working. A small boy in ragged shorts and a back-to-front baseball cap was sitting on a barrel and smoking the butt of a cigar that somebody had probably thrown away.

'At a rough guess,' Morton said, 'half the guys you see here have committed crimes of one sort or another, mostly petty; and that could be a low estimate.'

'What do you do about it?'

'Now and then we pull some of them in.'

'But not all?'

'If we did that,' Morton said, 'there just wouldn't be room in the old jailhouse.'

Before leaving the harbour area they came upon an incident. Morton spotted a police patrol car drawn up at the entrance to a bar, where a small crowd had gathered.

'Something's happening,' he said. 'Might be interesting. Let's go take a look.'

He stopped the car by the kerb and they both got out. Morton shouldered his way through the bystanders and Devon followed him into the bar. It was just a long narrow room with a counter along one side and a few tables and chairs, some of them overturned. There must have been some twenty or thirty men and women in there, and all of them seemed to be talking at once at the top of their voices. A couple of uniformed police-men were doing their best to control the hubbub, but they were not having much success.

The reason for the commotion was obvious at once. A man was lying on the floor and bleeding from several stab wounds. He was not dead, but he appeared to be in a pretty bad way and was moaning. Another man, whose shirt was spattered with blood, was in handcuffs, and there was blood on his hands too. A bloodstained knife was lying on the floor and there were no prizes for guessing who had been using it.

Morton spoke to one of the policemen. 'What happened?'

The policeman evidently knew him. He said: 'The usual. Two guys get to arguin'; one of 'em hauls out a blade and lets the other have it in the chest.'

'What was the argument about?'

'Seems like it was a woman. Her up against the bar.'

Devon glanced at the woman indicated by the policeman. He would not have said she was worth fighting over. There was a blowsy look about her and she was certainly not young. She seemed to be taking the whole business with remarkable coolness; she had one elbow on the bar and was smoking a cigarette. Her expression was one of disdain, as though she found the proceedings rather distasteful and perhaps a trifle ridiculous. She was certainly shedding no tears over the man on the floor, and she appeared unconcerned about the one in handcuffs as well.

Two more policemen arrived, and then an ambulance. The injured man was carried out on a stretcher, still moaning piteously.

'Let's go, Frank,' Morton said. 'Nothing here for us to do. The boys can handle this.'

The small crowd outside had already melted away. The brief excitement was over. Morton and Devon got back into the Rover.

'Think the man will live?' Devon asked.

'Doubtful. Looked a goner to me. Fifty-fifty chance maybe.'

'You get much of this sort of thing?'

'Happens all the time. Usually later in the day. Guys get the rum inside them an' they jus' go crazy.'

'Over women?'

'Not always. There's other things make them mad. But mostly it's dames. Sometimes it's the woman go crazy over her man; 'nother woman give him that certain look and she for it. Yes, sir. Jealousy, jealousy! My, oh my!'

Morton sounded faintly amused, faintly contemptuous of such weakness. Devon wondered whether he himself had ever been troubled by that green-eyed monster. It was not a question he felt it advisable to ask on so short an acquaintance.

They left the town and drove into the hinterland where the road climbed tortuously towards the hills that were green with vegetation. Here and there were patches of sugar-cane, citrus trees, bananas hanging in clusters, bread fruit. In places branches overhung the road, so that they seemed to be going through a living tunnel; at one point a stream tumbled down a rocky slope, scattering spray that glittered in the sunlight.

There was not much traffic: a few lorries, some cars, now and then a donkey cart or a pack mule, once a group of women with wide shallow baskets on their heads and children trailing behind, an old man on an old bicycle.

They did not go far. They came back to the town past some very fine houses built on the higher ground away from the harbour and the squalor of the shanties, having large gardens and set well back from the road.

'Some people must have plenty of money to live in these places,' Devon remarked. 'Who owns them and how do they get to be so rich?'

'Good question,' Morton said. But he made no attempt to answer it. Perhaps he did not know the answer.

'I thought this was a poor island.'

'Maybe it is. And maybe even in islands like this there's ways of pulling in the shekels if you have the know-how. And no conscience to put the brakes on what you're doing.'

'Are you telling me these people are crooks?'

'No,' Morton said, 'I'm not telling you that.'

Yet it was what he seemed to be hinting at. And of course, there were ways of enriching oneself which, even if they were not strictly speaking illegal, yet bordered on that shadowy area and might have been rejected by a person of uncompromising integrity. Maybe St Joseph was a tax haven and maybe some of these desirable properties were owned, not by indigenous islanders but by wealthy expatriates determined to hang on to the bulk of those treasures which they had acquired by one means or another, fair or foul.

Anyway, it was none of his business and he decided not to bother himself about it.

*

It was evening when they finally arrived at Morton's own home. It was a timber bungalow of modest proportions, and there were other properties of a similar size to the right and the left of it; even more of the same on the opposite side of the road. Darkness had fallen, so that Devon was seeing the place only by lamplight, but he was able to see that there was a small garden in front, with mown grass and a few shrubs. At one side was a strip of concrete on which Morton parked the car. They both got out and he led the way to the front door.

Then was a tiny entrance hall, and suddenly it was full of human beings giving them a great welcome. Devon wondered whether Morton was always greeted so enthusiastically when he arrived home or whether this was a special occasion because of the stranger in their midst. Either way, it was certainly pleasant.

Morton did the introducing. His wife, Ida, was not the lean type like her husband; she had probably put on a good deal of weight since her youth, but she was certainly not obese. There were some flecks of grey in her hair, and she might have been a year or two older than Duke.

She gave Devon a big smile and said how pleased she was to meet him. She also said she just hoped he would feel at home. He already did; it would have been impossible not to in that house.

There were two children, a boy and a girl. Mark was ten and

Maria was eight. They were a little shy at first, but the shyness did not last long.

'Is it true,' Mark said, 'that you're a London cop?'

'Yes, it's true.'

'My!'

It was the first time Devon had encountered such wide-eyed wonder at this simple fact. No other person, as far as he could remember, had ever appeared at all impressed by the nature of his employment.

'It's just a job, you know.'

But not for this boy perhaps. His father was also a cop, but he operated here, close to home on this small West Indian island. London was far away, one of the great cities of the world; it had a glamour that Arthurton could not match.

There was a fourth person to be introduced to. She was standing a little behind the others. Devon already knew her name; it was Jessica. Morton had told him this. He had also told him that Jessica was a widow and that her married name was Brown. She was his sister, and she had been widowed when her husband, Rory Brown, had been drowned on a fishing trip with another man named Tait. Their boat had been caught in a freak storm and had capsized. The incident had been witnessed by some men in another boat, but they had been unable to give any aid and felt lucky to have survived themselves. Since her bereavement, which had taken place about a year ago, Jessica had been living with her brother and his family.

Devon, therefore, had been expecting to meet the widow and

had had a picture in his mind of a woman of around Morton's own age, possibly rather stout and with no pretensions whatever to any physical beauty. What he realized now was that this mental picture could not have been further off the mark. Morton had indeed told him something about this sister of his but he had not told it all. What he had omitted to say was that she was a lot younger than him; not much over twenty, Devon would have guessed; and that she was a real beauty, no doubt about that.

She was not as dark as her brother; brown rather than black, with a velvety skin and hair piled up in tight little curls that glistened in the lamplight. Her eyes reminded him of Christine's; they had that same dark lustre, a kind of melting quality that he found enchanting. She was rather tall for a woman and slender; there were queens of the catwalk earning fabulous amounts of money who were not nearly as attractive. Not to him; certainly not to him.

She said nothing. She just looked at him and smiled. But such a smile!

He said: 'This is nice; this is really nice. It makes me just glad to be here. I didn't expect such a welcome. I could be a VIP.'

'In this household,' Morton said, 'believe me, you are.'

They had the meal in an L-shaped room which was part kitchen and part dining-room. The food was first class, and Devon complimented Ida on her cooking.

He could see that it pleased her, but she said that she could not take all the credit.

'I have a real good assistant,' she said; and she glanced at Jessica.

'She could do it just as well without my help,' Jessica said. 'She's the tops.'

Ida gave a shake of the head as if to repudiate such high praise, but again she looked pleased.

'How long are you going to stay on the island, Frank?' Jessica asked.

He told her that according to the plan he was to be there for three months.

'I do hope you'll like it here.'

'Judging by first impressions,' Devon said, 'I have no doubt at all that I shall.'

Morton took him back to the chalet and said he would call for him in the morning. He hoped Devon would sleep well.

'Like a log,' Devon said.

'Anything more I can do for you right now?'

Devon shook his head. 'You've given me a soft landing as it is. Thanks a lot, Duke.'

'Know something?' Morton said. 'I reckon we'll make a good team, you an' me. What you say?'

'I think the same.'

'Well, goodnight, Frank.'

'Goodnight, Duke.'

Chapter Four

SOMETHING OF INTEREST

He slept well and woke refreshed. He took a shower and had just got himself dressed when there was a knock at the door. He had not expected Morton quite so early but could think of no one else it could be at that hour, or any hour if it came to that. There was, however, one sure way of finding out who it was, and he walked to the door and opened it. He was surprised to see Jessica Brown standing on the verandah that ran along the front of the chalet.

'Hi there, Frank,' she said. 'I hope I'm not too early.'

She was in shorts and a T-shirt, and there was a bicycle leaning against the verandah, so it was not difficult to guess that she had ridden over from Morton's place on the machine. But why she had seen fit to do so was a mystery.

'Too early for what?' he asked.

She smiled. 'What I meant was, I didn't get you out of bed or anything, did I?'

'No, not anything. But I still don't understand why you're

here. You haven't brought a message from Duke, have you?'

'Well no, not exactly. But he was the one who suggested it.'

She paused, and Devon thought she seemed just a trifle embarrassed. So he did a little prompting.

'Suggested what, precisely?'

'That you might need someone to do the chores, keep the place tidy, wash your clothes, maybe do a bit of cooking, that sort of thing.'

'I see. And then I suppose he also suggested that you might apply for the job?'

'Well, yes. But of course if you don't want anyone you've only got to say the word. Tell me to beat it and I'll go.'

It had not occurred to him that he would need any help of this kind, but now that it had been suggested to him he saw that it was not at all a bad idea; in fact it seemed a very good one. And it had to be admitted that one of the reasons – and maybe the chief reason of all – for coming to this conclusion was the fact that the person putting in for the position of housekeeper was none other than the altogether charming Mrs Jessica Brown. It took him only a very few seconds to decide to accept the offer and welcome the applicant with the greatest of pleasure. Only a confirmed misogynist could have brought himself to turn her away, and he was most certainly not of that breed.

'You'd better come inside,' he said.

She looked pleased. 'Does that mean I've got the job?'

'I think it's something we should have a talk about,' Devon said. But he knew already where the talking would lead. It was a foregone conclusion that she would soon be working for him, and he was happy that she would.

They went in, and he had a feeling that she was no stranger to the interior of the chalet.

'You've been in here before, haven't you?' he said. 'It was you who got the place ready for me.'

She admitted that it was. 'Somebody had to do it. It was such a mess. Nobody's lived here for months; maybe a year. The project was a failure, you know.'

'Yes. Duke told me.'

'Have you had breakfast?' she asked.

'No.'

'Would you like me to cook something?'

'Don't bother.'

'Be no bother. Just say the word.'

She seemed quite eager for the word, but he did not give it. 'A plate of cereal will do for me. I'm not one for a heavy first meal of the day.'

'Well, please yourself,' she said. 'You'd like coffee?'

'Coffee would be fine.'

She made it in a percolator, the real thing, not instant; and she drank a cup herself to keep him company. While he was eating she sat at the opposite end of the table, and now and then he would find her gazing at him rather intently, as though she were somehow sizing him up. Then when he caught her eye her gaze would slide away and she would look slightly embarrassed at being detected in this examination of him.

'Well?' he said. 'Do I pass?'

'Pass?'

'I think you've been weighing me up, haven't you?'

She gave one of her enchanting smiles. 'Oh, I did that yesterday. I've just been checking the reading.'

'And what does it say?'

'It says you're probably okay.'

'Only probably? That's rather disappointing.'

'Well,' she said, 'it's early days yet, isn't it?'

Morton turned up later. They heard the sound of his footsteps on the verandah, and then he knocked and walked in.

'You two come to an agreement?' he asked.

'I think it was all arranged for me,' Devon said. 'I just had to give the nod.'

'You could still say no.'

'And what would you think if I did that?'

'Think you was crazy.'

'I'm not crazy,' Devon said.

Morton grinned. 'I guess not.'

They drove away in Morton's car, leaving Jessica in charge of the chalet. She had a key so that she could lock up when she had finished the chores. The question of how much she was to be paid for her services had been touched on briefly, but nothing had been settled. Both of them had rather shied away from that subject and it had been postponed to a later date.

Morton drove to police headquarters for orders, and while they were there a report came in of the finding of a dead body. There was nothing unusual in this; as Morton had told Devon, the murder rate on the island was high. But what made this particular case of more than ordinary interest was that the body was that of a white male. It was for this reason that Christy decided that Morton and Devon should take a hand in the investigation.

'Something of interest for our visitor from London to take a look at. Maybe you'll be able to give us some valuable help in the operation, sergeant. You may detect some priceless clue that would have escaped our dull West Indian eyes.'

Devon was conscious of a note of sarcasm in the fat man's voice, but he ignored it.

'Whatever you say, sir.'

It was apparent that the superintendent himself was not going to look at the body; it was doubtful whether he had bothered himself with that kind of chore for quite some time. A detective inspector named Christian Horler would be handling the case, and the two sergeants would merely be assisting him. Horler was a sad-faced middle-aged man who seemed to carry an air of disillusionment around with him. He probably knew that he had reached the peak of his career and would get no further promotion, and he was looking forward to the day when he came up to the age for retirement. Meanwhile he would go through the motions of his job with as little enthusiasm as he might have shown when sweeping up the rubbish in his own backyard.

Morton told Devon that Horler had been a pretty smart offi-cer at one time, but a year or two ago he had lost his wife and it had had a depressing effect on him.

'He just seemed to lose interest. Another year and he'll be out of it. He'll take his pension and go.'

The body had apparently been washed up on a beach on the north shore of the bay, just beyond the fringes of the town. It had been discovered by a man doing a bit of beachcombing. There had been no one else about at the time. This man, a ragged old character called Wandering Willy, was still around when Morton and Devon arrived on the scene, preceded by Detective Inspector Horler and a detective constable. They had had to leave the cars on a dirt road some hundred yards back from the beach. There was a patrol car already parked there. Then they had had to scramble down a fairly steep and crumbling bank before reaching the spot where the body was lying.

A couple of uniformed officers were already there, keeping at a distance some inquisitive bystanders who had appeared from nowhere and were carrying on a discussion among themselves. The officers were also making sure that Wandering Willy didn't take it into his head to wander off before the detectives had a chance to question him.

The dead man was lying on his back and was stark naked. He could not have been very long in the sea because the body was in pretty good condition. And one thing became obvious at a glance: he had not died by drowning. For nobody took a drowned man out of the water and drilled a tunnel through his cranium with a bullet. That would have been piling Pelion on Ossa.

The hole where the bullet had gone in was in the middle of the forehead, and it looked quite neat and tidy. As much could not be said for the hole at the back of the skull where it had come out; that was a very nasty piece of work indeed; jagged and gaping. But this was not at once apparent because for the present the back of the head was hidden in the sand.

Horler looked down at the body and gave a sigh. 'Dear, dear, dear, oh dear!'

He turned his head and looked towards the open sea, as though trying to guess just where the body had come from. Then he spoke to Wandering Willy.

'This is just where you found him?'

'Yes,' Willy said.

'You haven't touched the body?'

'No, no, no!'

'So then what did you do?'

'I run to tell the coppers.'

One of the uniformed men chipped in: 'That's right. We saw him on the road waving his arms like a madman. Picked him up and came back with him here.'

Horler turned to Willy again. 'Nobody else on the beach when you found the body?'

'I didn't see none.'

Horler looked down again at the corpse. 'Something odd here.'

'What's that?' Morton asked.

'Body's dry.'

'Could've dried in the sun. Wouldn't take long.'

'Or it might never have been wet.' He turned to Devon. 'What you think, sergeant?'

'I think it never was in the sea. If the water had dried on it there'd have been some salt on the skin. I don't see any.'

'There's some scum on it,' Morton said.

'It could have been lying there when the tide came in. This seems to be the tidemark right here where it is. A bit of foam maybe got on it and then the tide started going out again and left it there.'

'Sounds reasonable,' Morton admitted.

'Question is,' Horler said, 'was he brung down here from the road or did he come by boat?'

Devon looked back towards the bank down which they had scrambled. The sand in that direction had been churned up by several feet and it was impossible to say whether there were any footmarks that might have been made by men carrying a dead body. He took another look at the corpse and the sand around it.

'My money is on the boat.'

'How come?' Horler asked.

'Those footprints by the head, they're pointing up the beach but they don't lead anywhere; they're only here where the body was dumped. And there are more by the feet; they just don't connect with fresh ones. And besides, if you look, there's only one set of prints heading up the beach and they have to be Willy's. The two cops didn't go back to their car; they phoned from here on the mobile.'

Horler seemed doubtful as to whether this evidence was conclusive; the prints were none too well marked and the sand had been kicked up quite a lot, as it would have been by two men carrying a heavy weight between them. But there were also some prints pointing directly towards the sea and a few that had been only half obliterated by the advancing tide, which had then retreated.

'I think Frank's right,' Morton said.

'So why in hell did those guys in the boat go to the trouble of bringing him ashore? Why didn't they just shove him overboard in deep water? Been a lot easier.'

'Maybe they wanted to make sure he was found,' Devon suggested. 'Maybe that's why they left him above the tidemark.'

'Why would they want him found?'

'I don't know. As a warning, maybe.'

'A warning to who, for God's sake?'

'I've no idea. I'm just the new boy around here.'

Horler looked at him sourly. 'A new boy with plenty to say for himself.'

'I'm just trying to help.'

'Sure, sure,' Horler said grumpily. 'We're all very grateful.'

He turned to the detective who had come with him and told

the man to start taking photographs of the corpse with the camera he had brought with him.

'And make sure you get those footprints in.'

Two more men, dressed in white shirts and trousers, arrived soon after that with a stretcher. When the man with the camera had finished his work Horler gave them leave to take the body away.

It was hard work. The unknown dead man was no light weight and he had to be carried up the beach and over the bank to where an ambulance was waiting to transport him on his penultimate journey.

Devon asked Morton where they would be taking him, and Morton gave a wry grin.

'To the morgue. Where else?'

Chapter Five

IRRELEVANT

It was routine work. Some of it was done by uniformed officers and some by Morton and Devon, since it was Horler's case and they were Horler's assistants. They had photographs of the dead man's face, touched up a little so that the hole in the forehead was not visible, and they went round trying to find someone who recognised the subject.

It should have been easy. The man was white, so that put him in a small minority on the island. Yet in the event it was not easy, for as far as they could discover no white man had gone missing.

The known white residents on the island were soon checked up on and found to be all present and correct, so they could be ruled out. That left the holidaymakers, and the majority of these were congregated at Logan's Bay, which was on the west side of the island and about a dozen miles from Arthurton by way of the coast road.

Morton and Devon drove out there and started making inquiries. It was an idyllic spot: blue sea on one side and green hills on the other. The bay was small and almost perfectly circular in shape, with only a narrow opening to the sea between two rocky promontories. There were beaches of silver sand fringed with coconut palms, and there were a couple of hotels and a number of chalets and a few shops selling the kind of gear that people on holiday liked to spend their money on.

'Nice place,' Devon said. 'Wouldn't expect anybody to get murdered here.'

'If somebody wants to put a bit of lead in your brain,' Morton said, 'he'll do it anywhere, nice place or bad. Makes no difference. Let's make a start on the hotels.'

They drew a blank at the hotels; all guests were accounted for and no one was missing. Besides which, none of the employees had ever seen anyone who looked like the man in the photograph.

They moved on to the chalets. In several of them there was nobody at home. Where there was somebody they got the same result, a shake of the head. There were not even any doubters who thought they might have seen someone who looked like the man; they were all certain they had not.

They combed the beach, accosting one person after another; and there too they drew a blank. They could not be sure that they had questioned everyone, but the number of holidaymakers was not great, and if one of them had mysteriously vanished it would surely have been generally known. Someone would have been searching frantically for a husband or companion or boyfriend. But there was no such panic at Logan's Bay, that was certain.

'My bet is he was no holidaymaker,' Devon said. 'Where would have been the point in killing someone like that and dumping the body on a beach? Doesn't make sense.'

Morton was inclined to agree. 'There's got to be a strong motive. Ain't the kinda thing you do on the spur of the moment.'

'True. Get the motive and we're halfway there.'

'Trouble is we ain't even halfway to finding it. I'd say we're all washed up here and might as well go home.'

They returned to Arthurton and switched their inquiries to the ships in the harbour. Same questions, same answers: no crew member gone missing; no knowledge of anyone who looked like the man in the photograph.

Evening came and the investigation had led to no result in any quarter. No clue of any sort had been discovered and Horler was pessimistic.

'Dead end,' he said. 'Dead end.' And Devon was sure he was not making a joke with this play on words. He doubted whether Detective Inspector Christian Horler ever made jokes; it was not in his character.

Detective Superintendent Christy was philosophical about the lack of progress; it did not appear to bother him greatly. Possibly he was used to murder investigations that ended in failure.

'Some you win, some you lose. We'll stick at it for a time. Something may turn up. If not—' He gave a lift of his massive shoulders which said it all. He was not going to lose any sleep over just another stiff, even if the stiff was a white one.

Devon had dinner again with the Morton family. He had protested that he could not continue imposing himself on them, but Morton had insisted that it was no imposition and that everyone was expecting him.

'They can't have enough of you, Frank. That's the way it is. It's like you're the flavour of the month.'

'It's just the novelty. It'll wear off in a little while. You'll see.'

'Maybe so. But right now you're in demand. So why not make the most of it while it lasts?'

The welcome was as unreserved as it had been the previous day. And the meal was as good. It was better than the lunch they had had in the canteen at police headquarters, though that had been perfectly adequate. The company there had not been the same of course, and that made a difference. Morton's kids were still idolising him, and for them the novelty was certainly showing no signs yet of wearing off. But it had to be remembered that this was only the second day of his stay on the island.

Jessica was there. She was in a dress now, not the shorts and T-shirt she had been wearing when he had left her at the chalet in the morning. He was pleased to see her again. It rather surprised him to find just how pleased he was. She looked pleased too.

'Have you had a good day?' she asked.

'It's been interesting,' he said. He avoided mentioning the murder investigation. If Morton wished to talk about it he could, but maybe he never discussed such matters with the family.

He was wrong about this.

Morton said: 'We've been working on a murder case. Dead white man on the north beach. Identity unknown.'

Jessica looked at Devon. 'So you've been pitched in at the deep end straightaway.'

'Looks like it.'

'You going to find the killer, Frank?' Mark asked.

Devon smiled. 'I'm just an assistant. I'm not in charge of the investigation.'

'But you're a London cop.'

'That doesn't mean I'm infallible. We don't solve all our mysteries even over there. Far from it.'

'But you'll solve this one. You will, won't you?'

Ida Morton said: 'Now that's enough, Mark. Don't badger our guest. Let's talk about something else, shall we?'

'But—'

'Mark!'

That silenced him. Ida Morton might seem easy-going but it was apparent that she had authority in her own home. The subject of the murder investigation was dropped from the conversation and cricket took its place. Mark sulked for a minute or two, but then brightened up again. He couldn't stay silent for long.

'You ever been to Lord's, Frank?'

'Many times,' Devon said. 'And the Oval.'

'My! You play cricket?'

'A bit.'

'You play at Lord's?'

'No, I'm not in that class. Do you play?'

'Yes, At school.'

'He's a batsman,' Morton said. 'Some day he reckon to play for West Indies.' He gave a grin.

'Is that so, Mark?'

'I'd like,' the boy said.

'He's a left-hander,' Morton said.

'Oh, like Brian Lara and Gary Sobers.'

'Thinks he will be some day,' Maria said. She herself seemed to have doubts.

'Well, maybe he'll make it. What do you say, Mark?'

'St Joseph never had a Test player,' the boy said.

'There's a first time for everything. Now here's a promise. You get to play at Lord's and I'll come and watch. Cheer too. Even if you make a century against England.'

The boy laughed. 'It's deal.'

Morton drove him back to the chalet and promised to pick him up in the morning at the usual time.

'Maybe tomorrow we'll get a lead,' Devon said.

'I wouldn't bet on it. This one seems like a real mystery to me. But you never know.'

'Horler seems to be pessimistic about it.'

'Well, that's old Christian for you.'

'Is he always like that?'

'You bet. He won't be happy till he's finished his time and is out of it for good.'

'You think he'll be happy then?'

'Hell, no,' Morton said; and he gave a laugh.

'Christy doesn't seem bothered.'

'Only thing that'd bother him,' Morton said, 'is if he didn't get his meals reg'lar.'

Devon reflected that it hardly looked as if they were going to be much pressed to achieve a result. So perhaps that was the way of things on the island; perhaps they took life easy. And death too. Even the violent kind.

In which case why should he worry? It was no skin off his nose if a murder mystery went unsolved. So why not treat his stay in St Joseph as a holiday and simply go through the motions? It might turn out to be quite an enjoyable break from the old routine.

He thought of Jessica, whom he would be seeing every day, and that was no unpleasant thought. Yes indeed, this could be a most delightful change from his duties back home in London.

And the body on the beach? Well, to hell with that. It was not going to spoil anything for him. In relation to his non professional activities on this enchanting tropical island it was completely irrelevant.

At least, that was what he told himself.

Chapter Six

THE MORGUE

They picked up a paper on the way to work in the morning. It was the *St Joseph Telegraph*, the only daily paper on the island. There was a report of the finding of the dead body on the beach. It stated that the victim was a white male, that he had been shot in the head and had not yet been identified. It said also that the police were baffled, which was a good old reporter's term, but that they were following up certain lines of inquiry – which was the kind of statement the police usually handed out when they were baffled.

'You know anything about those lines, Duke?' Devon asked.

'Search me,' Morton said. 'Sounds like something Christy fed to them.'

When they checked in at headquarters they found Horler in a black mood. He had toothache, and this seemed to have made him even gloomier than usual. Devon thought this was not surprising; he had never yet met anyone who could suffer a bad attack of toothache with any degree of cheerfulness. Horler's face was swollen and it looked as if he had a gumboil.

'I'm going to see the dentist,' he said. 'You two'll have to take care of things without me.'

'What do you want us to do?' Morton asked.

'I don't give a damn what you do,' Horler told him sourly. 'Use your initiative. If you've got any.'

He went away, muttering to himself.

The police surgeon's report had come in. The victim's age was reckoned to be about thirty-five. He was five feet ten inches in height, weight one hundred and seventy-two pounds. Death was the result of being shot through the head, probably with a handgun of large calibre. Burn marks on the forehead indicated that the gun had been fired at very close range. The man had been dead for no more than twenty-four hours and there was no indication that the body had ever been immersed in sea-water.

'Doesn't tell us much we didn't already know,' Devon said. 'So what now?'

'Wanna take a look at the morgue?'

It sounded as good a suggestion as any, though taking another look at the body was hardly likely to give them any sudden inspiration. It would just be a way of filling in time.

'Might as well.'

'Let's go then.'

The morgue was a plain white building of one storey, tucked away at the end of a cul-de-sac. There were two cars standing in front of it, and Morton parked the Rover nearby. As he and Devon walked towards the entrance to the morgue a man came out and strolled across to one of the parked cars. He was white and he was dressed in khaki slacks and a bushshirt, a pair of scuffed leather boat shoes on his feet. He was maybe a shade under six feet in height and lean, and he could have been in his late thirties. He had a craggy tanned face and he was wearing a floppy old sun-hat, frayed at the brim, under which some straw-coloured hair was visible. He glanced at the two detectives in passing, but said nothing.

Devon got the impression of a hard-bitten individual; someone who would likely know how to take care of himself in a tough situation.

'Now what in hell was he doing here?' Morton said.

'You know him?'

'Never saw him before.'

The man had got into his car and was driving away. They watched him go.

'Well, let's go inside and take a look at the corpse,' Morton said. 'Not that it'll do much good.'

Devon had never liked morgues, and he had been in a few of them in the course of his police career. They were depressing places and he wondered how the people who worked in them stood it. All that work with dead bodies; it was enough to drive you round the bend or into a state of permanent melancholia. Yet he had never found such individuals any less cheerful than the general run of the population. Indeed, some of them seemed to have an air of jollity about them and a macabre sense of humour. Well, it took all sorts.

There was a distinct chill in the place, contrasting sharply with the warmth outside, as though the air-conditioning had got out of hand. And there was that odour, hard to describe it but somehow nauseating; at least to him. Not the odour of death but of preservation. And the whiteness everywhere; the walls, the ceiling, the coats of the attendants, whose black faces and hands seemed like an intrusion.

The man who pulled out the long drawer containing the corpse was known to Morton, who addressed him as Joe. He was fat and round-faced and seemed happy in his work.

'Here we are,' he said. 'Here's your boy.'

Their boy lay in his narrow bed, eyes closed, unmoving. He looked little different from the way he had looked the previous day on the beach. They had not expected much change, and in his present position he offered no more clue to the mystery of his death than he had before. If they were seeking in this cold slab of human flesh and bone some sudden inspiration that would set them on the track of the killer, they were doomed to disappointment. But they had expected nothing, and nothing was what they got.

'If you could only speak,' Morton said, 'what a tale you might have to tell.'

'If dead men could speak,' Devon said, 'our job would be a sight easier.'

But the corpse was saying nothing.

'Shove him back in, Joe,' Morton said.

The man in the white coat slid the drawer into its recess and the body vanished from sight.

'That guy who left just before we arrived,' Morton said. 'You see him?'

'Oh, yes.'

'What'd he want?'

'Same as you.'

'He wanted to take a look at the cadaver?'

'That's right.'

'Why?'

'Thought he might recognise it.'

'And did he?'

'No.'

'You show your dead bodies to anyone who just happens to walk in and ask you to?'

Joe looked uncomfortable. 'Well, no. Didn't seem no harm in it, though. Seemed to be a nice enough guy.'

'How much did he pay you?'

'Well—'

'Okay, Joe. Don't tell me. None of my business. But you better watch your step. You could get yourself into trouble.'

Devon was glad to leave the morgue and step out into the fresh air and the sunshine.

'That white guy,' Morton said thoughtfully. 'Wonder who he was. Odd thing that. Why'd he think he might recognize the stiff?'

'Beats me,' Devon said. 'Anyway, he didn't.'

'That's what he said.'

'You think he could have been lying?'

'I'd say it's a possibility. And how'd he know about the dead guy anyway?'

'It's in the paper,' Devon said. 'Could've read about it. Or he could've heard it from one of the people we questioned yesterday.'

'We didn't tell them the man was dead.'

'Things like that get round.'

'Guess so.'

That same day, just after they had had lunch in the canteen, they received a summons to Detective Superintendent Christy's office.

'Ah,' the big man said as they walked in, 'there you are. How's that murder investigation coming along?'

'We're still making inquiries, sir,' Morton said.

'And getting nowhere fast, I've no doubt.'

'Could take time.'

'You think you can crack it eventually?'

'We can try, sir.'

'Don't.'

Morton and Devon stared at him.

'Don't try, sir?' Morton said. 'Is that what you mean?'

'Right in one. We're closing the book on this one. Dropping the investigation.'

'Already? But why?'

'Waste of time. Not enough to go on. Better things for you to do with your time. That'll be all.'

He gave a gesture of dismissal and they left his majestic presence.

'I don't understand this,' Devon said. 'Does he usually give up on a case as easily as this?'

'No.' Morton said. 'And my guess is he's had orders from higher up. I'd say there's more to this than meets the eye.'

'Like what?'

'Good question. But I don't know the answer. Anyhow, that's the way it is.'

'And a damned strange way it is too, if you ask me.'

Morton grinned. 'Not the way you do things in London?'

'No.'

'Well, you ain't in London now.'

'That's for sure,' Devon said.

The following evening he took the whole Morton family out to dinner. He felt it was the least he could do by way of some return for the meals he had had in their house, though both Duke and Ida protested that it was not at all necessary.

He consulted Morton as to the best place to choose, and Morton suggested a restaurant called The Buccaneer, which was on Market Street, where the best shops were. It was a good choice; the restaurant was not particularly large, but it had air-conditioning, which made it pleasantly cool. The cuisine turned out to be top class and the service was excellent; so all in all things could hardly have been better. The children were on their best behaviour, which Devon noted with approval; he had seen too many badly brought up little darlings making themselves thorough pests in public places.

They were halfway through the meal when he caught sight of a man sitting by himself at a table on the far side of the room. He was some distance away and there were several tables in between the two of them, but Devon had a feeling that it was the man who had been leaving the morgue as he and Morton arrived on their visit. He could not be certain; other people's heads kept getting in the way, so that he had only an intermittent sight of the man, but he felt pretty well convinced that it was the one. Without the sun-hat to conceal it, more of the straw-coloured hair could be seen, receding somewhat from a bronzed forehead. And then the man looked across the room and for a moment their eyes met. He felt sure then that the recognition had been mutual.

Discreetly he drew Morton's attention, keeping his voice low.

'There's a man over there to your right. I think he's the one we saw at the morgue.'

Morton glanced in the direction indicated.

'You could be right,' he said.

'So what do we do about it?'

'Nothing.'

'You don't think one of us should go across and speak to him?'

'No,' Morton said. 'We're off duty and that case is closed anyway. Even if it is the same man, which ain't by no means certain, we've got no more interest in him. Leave it, Frank, leave it. Enjoy your meal. You're paying.'

'Now what are you two men whispering about?' Ida said. 'You're like a pair of conspirators.'

'Nothing,' Morton said. 'Nothing at all.'

'You often talk about nothing at all, Frank?'

'All the time,' Devon said. 'It's a most interesting subject. Didn't you know?'

When he looked across the room again the man with the straw-coloured hair had gone.

Chapter Seven

DOMESTIC

A couple of days after the dinner at The Buccaneer Morton and Devon were dispatched to deal with a rather unusual matter. A call for help had come through from the house of a Mr Jorge Ramirez. A woman had rung up, and it was difficult to make out just what she was saying because her English was not too good; in fact it was very bad indeed. But she sounded extremely excited, and frightened too; and as far as could be made out she was saying that some kind of mayhem was taking place and would someone come pretty damn quick and sort it out. And then her voice rose even higher and this time there was no mistaking the words even if the pronunciation was not all that hot.

' 'E keel 'er! 'E keel 'er!'

It was not certain who was killing whom, but before any elucidation could be obtained on that point a man's voice broke in with a stream of invective, or what might have been invective, though it was hard to tell for certain because it was in a language that was probably Spanish. And then there was the sound of a blow and a scream and a rattling noise and the line went dead.

It all sounded very much like a domestic drama, and in the ordinary way a patrol car would have been directed to the place with a couple of uniformed officers to deal with the matter. But apparently there was something special about this one, for the gist of the telephone call was passed immediately to higher authority and none other than Superintendent Calthorpe Christy summoned Morton and Devon to his presence and dispatched them to the house of Mr Ramirez with strict instructions to handle the matter with the utmost delicacy.

'Mr Ramirez is an important man, and we can't have any blundering policemen upsetting him. This is probably nothing more than a storm in a teacup, but it must be investigated; we can't just ignore the call. Still, I'm sure you two men have enought savvy to smooth things out. You get my meaning? Kid gloves, kid gloves and no mailed fists. That's the ticket.'

'Does that mean that if we find he's killed somebody – his wife for instance – we're just to slap his wrist and tell him not to do it again, sir?' Devon asked.

Christy looked annoyed. 'You know damn well that's not what I mean. I'm just telling you to use some tact and not go blowing this thing up outa all proportion. If you ain't up to handling it maybe Sergeant Morton'd better leave you here and see to it on his own. Is that what you'd like?'

'No, sir,' Devon said. 'I think I understand what's expected of us.'

'I hope so. I just hope so. Now get the hell outa here and on your way.'

'What got into you back there?' Morton asked when they were on their way. 'You crazy or something?'

'You think I shouldn't have said what I did?'

'Well,' Morton said, 'seems to me it wasn't exackly a good example of that tact and understanding we're supposed to use on this Ramirez guy. Now was it?'

'Maybe not. But what the devil is it with our Mr Ramirez? Why does he rate the kid glove treatment?'

'Now that's a real good question.'

'And you don't know the answer.'

'Not sure that I do, Frank, not sure that I do.'

'Or if you do, you're not telling me? Is that it?'

Morton said nothing.

'Is there anything you can tell me about him?' Devon asked. 'Just to put me in the picture.'

'Yes. He comes from Colombia and he's filthy rich.'

'Ah! Now that is interesting,' Devon said.

And he got to thinking that there had to be a very good reason why a Colombian who was filthy rich would want to come and live on a tiny little island like St Joseph. Was he perhaps running away from something? Like maybe one or two people who would have been glad to see him stretched out in one of those long narrow drawers in the Arthurton morgue like that mystery man who had been found on the beach with a hole in the head. Maybe.

When they came to the place he had additional reason for suspecting that Mr Ramirez might be running away from something or someone. Or rather not running but holed up in a pretty safe retreat where there would have been some difficulty in getting at him. Because the property was quite a fortress in its way.

It was up in the hilly part behind the town, and to get to it one had to drive along a narrow winding road, from which if you looked back there was a fine view across the bay. The ground on which the house stood was fairly level; it was like a wide shelf which might well have been scooped out of the hillside by mechanical diggers, though all evidence of this development work had become obliterated by the rapid growth of shrubs and ornamental trees and stretches of carpet-like lawn.

There was a stone wall surrounding the place, and a pair of tall wrought-iron gates ensured that no one could drive freely in or out. Along the top of the wall was a coil of razor wire which might have been electrified for extra security.

'Visitors not welcome,' Devon remarked. 'It seems our Mr Ramirez believes in keeping himself to himself.'

'Maybe with good reason.'

'And it's my experience that people who need to fence themselves in like this aren't usually the most law-abiding citizens in the world. My guess is he's a crook.'

'I'll tell you whether I agree with you on that point after I've had a look at the guy,' Morton said. 'Me, I'm keeping an open mind. Man's innocent till he's proved guilty. Ain't that so?'

'Only in theory,' Devon said. 'There's people going around as free as birds, and they're guilty as hell. They just happen to have smart lawyers – and the money to pay them. Billionaires can get away with murder – and often do.'

Morton pulled the car to a halt at the gates and gave a toot on the horn. There was a gatehouse just inside the perimeter wall, and a man came out and walked to the gates. He was swarthy and hard-faced with the kind of heavy jowl that needs shaving twice a day. He had a bushy moustache and he was wearing green cotton trousers and shirt, with some kind of badge on the chest. A wide leather belt with a brass buckle supported on the right hand side a holster with a big revolver in it. The man walked with a swagger, thumbs hooked in the belt, eyes wary.

He reached the gate and peered through the bars. He said something in a harsh gravelly voice. The language might have been Spanish.

Morton leaned out of the car and said: 'You speak English?'

'Yes,' the man said, grudgingly, as though it pained him to admit the fact. 'What you want?'

'To see Mr Ramirez. Police.' Morton produced his warrant card and showed it as proof. 'Had a call come through. Some trouble up at the house, so it seems.'

'No trouble I hear of,' the gatekeeper said.

'Well maybe you don't hear too good. Anyway, we had the message. You goin' to let us in?'

'I ask Mr Ramirez,' the man said, still grudgingly. 'You wait here.' He walked back to the gatehouse and went inside.

'Where in hell else did he expect us to wait?' Morton said. 'See that gun he had? Got no right tootin' it around. But rich men's bodyguards, they a law unto themselves. Do just what they please.'

The swarthy man remained inside the gatehouse, but suddenly there was a clicking sound and the gates swung inward of their own volition. It was evident that they were controlled electrically and that the man had been on the telephone to Ramirez and received the go-ahead.

Morton drove the car in and the gates closed behind them. They were now on a wide driveway which took a curve to the right and brought them within sight of a palatial building constructed of white stone. In front of it were lawns kept green by sprinklers, interspersed with flower beds in riotous colour and pergolas festooned with rampant climbers and trailing vines.

'Looks like Mr Ramirez has a good gardener,' Morton remarked. 'He don't see to all this on his own, I'd say.'

'I think you could be right at that,' Devon said.

Morton stopped the car at the end of the drive, and they got out and walked the last part of the way to the front of the house. The approach was terraced, and there were steps leading up to an impressive portico. A wide front door was standing open, but before they could reach it a man came out to meet them. He was less swarthy than the gatekeeper, taller and leaner, his age perhaps in the mid-forties, black hair greying at the temples, nose aquiline, a thin-lipped mouth with one of those neatly trimmed moustaches that film stars used to wear in the early days of the cinema. In his mind Devon classified him as a handsome bastard; not a man he would have cared to have dealings with; one who would bear watching. When he spoke it was in good English but with a noticeable foreign accent.

'I am Jorge Ramirez, as I imagine you have already guessed.'

Morton agreed that they had.

'I am afraid, officers, you have had a wasted journey. I am sorry about that.'

Morton said: 'There was a phone call, sir. Sounded like somebody was bein' killed.'

Ramirez gave a laugh. 'I assure you no one has been killed. It is all a foolish mistake.'

'We had to investigate,' Morton said. 'Couldn't just ignore the call and do nothin'.'

'Yes, I suppose that is so. You are merely doing your duty and I would not wish to stand in your way. But who do you think it was who was being killed?' He spoke lightly, faintly mocking in tone. 'My dear wife, perhaps? Come; let us go and see if she is dead.'

He led the way along the portico and round to the side of the house where there was a wide expanse of patterned tiling which extended to a swimming-pool with all the usual furniture beside it: chairs, recliners, tables, sunshades, hammocks; enough accommodation for a large party of bathers. But there was no party; there was just one woman, lying on one of the recliners and apparently reading a book.

She was wearing a white bikini and dark glasses and a wide-brimmed straw hat which was tilted down low over her forehead. She had a fine body, with long suntanned legs and firm breasts. Devon would have made a guess that she was ten years or more younger than her husband, though it was difficult to judge with the sunglasses hiding her eyes and the hat pulled down low. But from what he could see he came to the conclusion that she was quite a beauty, a judgement which was confirmed when she lowered the book and turned her head towards the three men who were approaching her. However, she made no other movement and gave no sign of taking any great interest in the newcomers.

'These men,' Ramirez said, 'are police officers. They believe you may have been physically assaulted.'

'We did not say that,' Morton said.

'But I am sure it was in your minds. So please tell them, my dear, that no one has attacked you.'

'No one has attacked me,' the woman said. She spoke without expression, tonelessly, as though repeating a lesson.

Devon noticed that she did not ask why they should have believed she might have been attacked. She seemed to have no curiosity whatever on that point. Which was odd.

'Dolores has been out here for most of the morning,' Ramirez said. 'Have you not, my love?'

'Yes,' she said, again in that toneless, unemphatic manner, 'I have been here most of the morning.' And then, as though she felt that this bald statement required some elaboration, she added: 'Reading.'

'An interesting book, no doubt,' Devon said.

She made no answer to that. She just looked at him. He would have liked to ask her to remove the glasses. There was some discolouration of the skin at the side of the left eye, and he suspected that the glasses might be hiding more. He would not have ruled out the possibility that she had recently taken a blow on that part of her face, and that the blow might have been inflicted by the knuckles of a clenched fist.

'Well, gentlemen,' Ramirez said, 'I hope this convinces you that your suspicions were groundless.'

'Oh, sure,' Morton said.

'Let me say again how sorry I am that you have had a wasted journey.'

'Not entirely wasted,' Devon said. 'It was worth it just to take a look at a place like this. To see how the other half lives.'

Ramirez smiled. 'You like it?'

'I'm not sure. Maybe it's a bit too rich for my taste. A shade too ostentatious.'

The smile vanished from Ramirez's face and he frowned slightly. The words might have implied a criticism of his own taste, and he was certainly not a man to accept criticism of any sort without resentment.

Morton said: 'That woman who made the telephone call, sir. If we could just have a word with her—'

Devon thought for a moment that Ramirez was going to refuse, and maybe tell them to get to hell out of it. But if that had indeed been in his mind, he had second thoughts and said:

'Very well. Come this way.'

They left Dolores to get on with her reading and went into the house, where the opulence of the furnishing was in keeping with the exterior. Ramirez led the way to a room which might have served as an office or a study – if the man ever studied anything apart from his bank balance. He pressed a button and in a few moments a young black maid appeared as if by magic.

'Send Inez to me,' Ramirez said.

The maid went away and a little later an older woman appeared. She was stout and there was a half-Spanish, half-Indian look about her. She had a hook nose and coarse black hair like a horse's mane.

'This is Inez,' Ramirez said. 'She is our housekeeper. Her English is poor, so you will have to make allowances.'

'And she is the one who made the telephone call?' Morton said.

'Yes.' Ramirez spoke to the woman. 'These are police officers. They want to know why you made that call to them. You will please tell us the reason.'

'Don't know,' the woman mumbled.

'But you said someone was killing someone,' Morton said. She just looked at him.

'Who was being killed?'

She glanced at Ramirez, then at the floor, and mumbled again: 'Don't know.'

Ramirez said; 'She is not quite –' He put a finger to his temple. 'You understand?'

Devon understood very well that Ramirez was suggesting the woman was not quite right in the head. He did not believe it. Would a man like him have employed a half-wit as housekeeper? It was more probable that the woman had been instructed to say nothing more than this. Threats might well have been used to intimidate her.

After a few more abortive attempts to get some sensible answers to his questions Morton threw in his hand and Ramirez dismissed the woman. She lost no time in leaving the room, no doubt relieved to be spared any further ordeal.

'Now,' Ramirez said briskly, 'is there anything else?'

Morton shook his head. 'No, sir; there's nothing else. Thank you for your co-operation.'

The swarthy man had the gates open for them even before they reached the entrance; he must have been alerted by Ramirez on the telephone. Morton drove the car through and the gates swung shut again behind them.

'What you think, Frank?' Morton asked.

'I think Ramirez is a liar. I think he was beating hell out of his wife and that woman Inez tried to stop him by ringing the police. Then he scared the pair of them into denying everything.'

'I'd say you're probably right. But it ain't none of our business. It's domestic. And the golden rule is; never get yourself involved in that kinda merry-go-round. Leave it to them to sort out among themselves.'

'Oh, you're right about that. But I'd certainly like to know a bit more about our Mr Ramirez. I think there's a damn sight more to him than meets the eye.'

'You think he's a crook?'

'Yes. Don't you, now that you've seen him?'

'Oh, sure.'

'So what are you going to do about it?'

'Nothing,' Morton said. 'Not a damn thing.'

Devon wondered why he was not really at all surprised by this reply.

Chapter Eight

NO ANSWER

Devon decided to rent a car for his private use, because it would give him more freedom of movement in his time off duty. Morton thought it was a good idea and told him where he could get one on reasonable terms. In fact he took him there.

It was a garage with the usual array of pumps on the forecourt and a workshop at the rear. There was a showroom with some new cars for sale, and there was a shop where you could buy almost anything from a can of lubricating oil to a packet of peanuts. The rental cars were standing outside with some used ones with prices marked on the windscreens.

The proprietor was a genial lanky black with an engaging grin, who went by the name of Sam Mopes. He was well known to Morton, who said that as car dealers went he was reasonably honest. Mopes was not a big operator in the car hire line, but he had a Ford Escort that he thought might suit Devon. He said it was in very good order and as the rental was lower than Devon had expected to have to pay, he took it. Mopes said that if he was not satisfied with it for any reason he could bring it back and change it for a different one.

'We aim to please.'

'It's a good slogan,' Devon said.

He could find no fault with the Escort, and he was glad that he no longer had to rely on Morton to come out and fetch him from the chalet. He could now drive himself to work.

Jessica seemed pleased. She thought it had been a great idea to get his own transport. That way you could go wherever you wished whenever you wished, without having to rely on the public transport system, which was erratic to say the least.

'Somebody like you just has to have a car.'

He was not quite sure what she meant by somebody like him, but he agreed, and he asked her if she would like to go out with him one evening to give the car a try-out. She made no attempt to hide her delight at the suggestion and had no hesitation in accepting the invitation.

'I'd love it. I think it's just the thing.'

'So how about tonight? If you haven't anything else arranged.'

'Nothing,' she said. 'Tonight will be fine by me.'

This conversation took place in the morning before he left for work, and as he drove away from the chalet he had a feeling of elation such as he had not experienced for quite some time. It surprised him a little.

More from a sense of duty than anything else he had sent a card to Chris. It was a picture postcard with a view of the harbour, and he could not think what to write on it. 'Having a grand time. Wish you were here,' would hardly have been appropriate. He did not wish she was there, and the fact of the matter was that there was someone else much more in his mind than she was. In the end he just wrote: 'Getting into the swing of things. Very different kind of job from London. Love. Frank.' He did not mention the chalet or the fact that he had a home help.

Later he tried to get through to her a few times on the telephone, but he got no reply. So had she really and truly done what she had threatened? Had she left him? Somehow, he did not much care. If she had gone, so be it. He decided to make no more calls. Why bother? Why not accept the fact that he was free from her? Maybe it was better that way, all things considered.

He picked Jessica up at Morton's place. It was already dark, but he drove out of town and on to the coast road to the south end of the island, headlights probing the darkness.

'It's a nice car,' Jessica said. 'Are you pleased with it?'

'Yes, I'm pleased with it. I got it from a man named Sam Mopes. But I believe I told you that.'

'Yes, you did.'

'Odd sort of name, that.'

'It is, isn't it?'

'He didn't look like a moper. Pretty cheerful really.'

It was a banal conversation, he thought. But he could think of nothing much to say. She was not being exactly fluent either. He sensed a kind of tension. There had never been any at the chalet; there they had both been completely relaxed. It was different now; it was as if they both knew that relations between them had taken a fresh course, and neither was sure quite where it would lead.

He stopped the car at a place where there was room to take it off the road. There was no moon yet, but the sky was spangled with stars. With the lights switched off they could see a reflection of this starshine in the sea below them. It glittered and was never still.

'Now there's a picture,' he said.

'It is lovely, isn't it?'

He glanced at her, a shadowy form in the other seat; and he saw her head turn; and he put an arm out and drew her towards him and kissed her. Her lips were warm and she made no move to draw away.

'I've been wanting to do that,' he said, 'ever since I first saw you.'

She laughed softly. 'And I've been wanting you to. Why did you wait so long?'

Back in town they went to an open-air cinema. There were moths and other night-flying creatures flitting between the projector and the screen, casting their shadows on the action, but Devon hardly noticed; his mind was on other things. What, he wondered, was he letting himself become involved in? Was he crazy? Was he in love with this girl? Was he really in love with her? Maybe. And maybe not just maybe either.

The film was a re-run of 'Four Weddings and a Funeral', and it seemed to be going down well with the audience. They laughed a lot. Afterwards Jessica asked him whether life in England was really like that.

'Not in my experience,' Devon said.

'I'd like to go there some day,' she said. 'Don't expect I ever will.' She sounded wistful.

'Well, you never know. The most unexpected things have a way of happening.'

'So you think I might?'

'Why not?' he said. And he had this sudden vision of her going back with him, and knew that it was a vision he ought to cast once and for all out of his mind; because with it must come all sorts of complications, one of which went by the name of Christine Devon.

Jessica knew about Chris; he had made no secret of the fact that he was married. But she knew also that that marriage was on the rocks or likely to be; so maybe to her way of thinking he was free from any obligations in that respect. Maybe she thought he would be getting a divorce. Or maybe she had given no thought to it at all. Maybe she took life as it came and left the future to take care of itself. Perhaps that was the best way.

So again he said: 'Why not?'

And she laughed and said: 'Well, maybe. Who knows? I may get to be rich.'

'You're rich now,' Devon said. 'Rich in everything but money. You're young, you're healthy, you're beautiful and you're happy. At least, I think you are.'

'Well,' she said, 'you could be right at that or you could be wrong. But either way, money's the only thing that counts when you walk into a bank. You can't cash dreams.'

He had to admit that there was truth in that. It was a great pity, but that was the way it was.

They had a meal at a small restaurant, sitting by themselves in a booth, which gave them a feeling of intimacy.

'Duke told me,' she said, 'that you went to see a man named Jorge Ramirez.'

'That's so.' He was not surprised that Morton had spoken about it. He did not seem averse to talking shop when off duty. 'A man from Colombia.'

'Now there,' she said, 'is one really rich person.'

'You know him?'

'Oh no. But with a place like that and servants and all he's just got to be, hasn't he?'

'And you'd like that?'

'Who wouldn't?'

'Money isn't everything.'

She smiled. 'Now where have I heard that one before?'

'You don't believe it?'

'Of course I believe it. But if you've got money you can buy most of the other things.'

'Not happiness.'

'How do you know? Have you tried?'

'No, I've never had the chance. But I'll tell you something. In Britain we have what's called the National Lottery. You can buy a ticket for a pound and you pick a set of numbers. There are two draws a week and they're shown on TV with a lot of razzmatazz and all that sort of junk. The odds against your numbers coming up are astronomical, but almost every week someone becomes an instant millionaire, and often more than one. But does it make them happy? Well, maybe some of them; but there are a lot who find it just ruins their lives. They've never been used to that sort of money and they just can't handle it; it's too much for them.'

'I'd know how to handle it,' she said.

'And you think it would make you happy?'

'You bet.'

'Well, maybe it would. And maybe we'll never know, one way or the other.'

'Have you ever bought a ticket?' she asked.

Morton laughed. 'Every week when I'm in London. Every damn week. I never miss.'

'And have you ever won anything?'

'Not a cent.'

'So are you happy?'

'As of this moment,' he said, 'I couldn't be happier.'

'How come?' she asked, giving him a coquettish look.

'I'm with you.'

'And that makes you happy?'

'What do you think?'

'I think you must be crazy,' she said.

But he thought she looked happy too.

He bought a bottle of wine and drove back to the chalet. They drank some of the wine and talked. And then they drank some more wine and talked some more. And when it was late he said:

'I'd better take you home.'

She smiled and said: 'You don't have to, you know.'

'They'll wonder where you are.'

'I think,' she said, 'they'll know where I am.'

'Will they mind?'

She laughed. 'Why should they mind? I'm not a kid.'

'That's true,' he said. 'That's very true.'

And he was glad.

He woke in the night. And his hand moved and he found her there. And she woke also and murmured:

'I love you, Frank.'

'I love you too, Jess,' he said.

And he drew her to him and kissed her, and they made love again, and she said:

'I'm so happy now. Are you happy, Frank?'

'Never more so,' he said. 'Never more so.'

And again he asked himself where things were heading and how it would all end. In tears? Who could tell? What was it the old Persian tentmaker had said? 'Unborn tomorrow and dead yesterday, Why fret about them if today be sweet!' Well, for him today was sweet, so why not take it for what it was and look no further ahead?

She moved in with him the next day. He had wondered how the Mortons would take it. He had felt apprehensive on that score, but he need not have done so. They seemed to take it in their stride. Perhaps they had seen it coming even before he had.

'The kids will miss you,' he said.

'They'll get used to it. It's not as if I'll never be there. I'm not going to stay in the chalet all the time you're away at work, just twiddling my thumbs and waiting for you to come home. I've got my bike; I'll still be mobile.'

It seemed a perfect arrangement. From his point of view nothing could have been better. Now that she was living with him life truly was sweet; sweeter than it had been since those early days of his marriage to Chris. He wondered whether he deserved such luck; but what did deserving have to do with it? Sometimes it occurred to him that it was too good to last; that fate must surely have something nasty lined up for him as compensation. But that was sheer superstition. Just because some good thing had been granted you, it didn't mean that a bad one must inevitably follow.

Nevertheless, every now and then he would have this uneasy feeling that it was all too good to last, that life for him could not continue at this level of delight for long. It was not in the nature of things. And even if nothing bad happened during his stay on the island, at the end of that secondment he would have to go back to England and leave Jessica here.

Unless he took her with him.

Again that thought. Again that question: was it on? And again no answer. He would have to think about it. He would have to think long and hard about it. That was for sure.

Chapter Nine

A MYSTERY

Devon was off duty for the whole of the weekend, and they drove out to Logan's Bay on the Saturday and spent the morning on the beach. They took a swim in the sea and sunbathed on the sand and generally had a lazy time of it.

'Tell me, Frank,' Jessica said. 'When you were told about this posting to St Joseph did you have anything like this in mind? Honestly now, did you?'

'Honestly then, no, I didn't. Though the man who gave me my orders, a detective superintendent named Alfred Lee, did suggest it was going to be a holiday in the sun. But I think he was just sour because he wasn't coming here himself.'

'So why did they pick you for the job?'

'I don't know. Maybe they just wanted to get shot of me for a time. It was a piece of luck anyway.'

'Lucky for me too. Perhaps too lucky.'

'How do you mean?'

'I mean maybe it's all just too good to last. Maybe nobody's meant to be quite so happy. Maybe something's waiting just around the corner to spoil it all.'

'Forget it,' he said. 'Nothing's going to spoil this for us. Nothing.' But had he not had the same kind of thought? An odd coincidence, that. But not significant. 'You're just being super-stitious. Keep your fingers crossed and everything will turn out okay. And don't walk under any ladders.'

After a sandwich lunch they went back to the car and drove along the winding switchback of the coast road to the southern corner of the island. Here there was a small cove at the foot of fairly high cliffs. Inland from the cove the ground rose rather steeply and was a kind of wilderness left to its natural state. There appeared to be no attempt at cultivation and possibly the soil was not suitable.

Devon parked the car at the side of the road, and they got out and scrambled up the hillside to get a better view of the sea. They soon reached a spot from which they could look down on the cove and the almost unruffled sea beyond it.

'This really is a marvellous view,' Devon said. 'Have you been up here before?'

'Never.'

'But you've been on this side of the island?'

'A few times. But not often. I mean, there's nothing much to come for in the ordinary way. Arthurton is where it's all at.'

'Yes, I suppose it is. For you.'

He could see that she had a point. On a small island like St

Joseph Arthurton was the hub; it had everything; it was nearest thing there was to a great city. So why travel out to this side of the island where there seemed to be nothing to speak of?

Looking down on the cove, he could see that there was a small beach and a jetty with a couple of boats alongside it. There were two or three people moving about, but they did not have the look of holidaymakers; no one was lying on the sand and soaking up the sun. On one side was a kind of gully in the cliff that looked as though it might have been carved out by a torrent of water, though it was now dry. It appeared to be the only way of getting down to the cove, and even that rough track was fairly steep and could have been used only by someone on foot.

'Not exactly buzzing with life, is it?' Devon said. 'Do you know the name of it?'

'Oh yes. It's called Salt Cove.'

'Why Salt?'

'I've no idea. Somebody's name maybe. Anyway, the water is salt, isn't it?'

Devon laughed. 'Sea-water usually is. What would the people down there do for a living?'

'How would I know? Fishing maybe.'

'Yes, I suppose that's possible.'

But he could see no evidence of this activity. There seemed to be no nets lying around, and the boats did not look like fishing craft, though at that distance it was difficult to be sure. The men themselves looked very small.

Suddenly he heard the drone of aircraft engines; faint at first but growing louder. And the engines were certainly not jets. The sound was coming from the west, and soon he caught sight of the plane, which was quite low and appeared to be heading directly towards the island. It had a curious shape, and as it came nearer he could see that it had two radial engines set close inboard and level with the long strutted wings.

'Well now,' he said. 'Whatever have we here?'

'An aeroplane, that's what,' Jessica said. 'Have you never seen one before?'

'Never one like this.'

And yet there was something strangely familiar about it, as though he had in fact seen something like it somewhere or other. But where?

It came closer, the thunderous roar of the engines preceding it, and he saw that there was a curious attachment to each wing-tip. Then suddenly it came to him: the wing-tips were retractable floats and the central fuselage from which the struts reached upward to the wings was the hull of a flying boat. And he knew why it seemed familiar; it was because he had seen pictures of that sort of plane in an old aircraft recognition book. Moreover, it was not just any common or garden flying boat; it was an amphibian which could land and take off either on water or land. It was in fact a Catalina.

'I don't believe it,' he said. 'I just don't believe it. It can't be. It's not possible.'

'What don't you believe?' she asked. 'What's not possible?'

'This thing I'm seeing.'

'But why not? It's only an old aeroplane.'

'But not just any old plane. This shouldn't be here. It's an anachronism.'

For the Catalina had been a World War Two aircraft. It had a long range and it did great work escorting convoys and other jobs of that sort. But that had been more than half a century ago. And even if some were still being built after the war ended, it could surely not have been for long. So this plane, if it was indeed a Catalina – and the closer it came the more certain he was of the fact – had to be very very old.

So was it possible? Was it really possible?

And the answer was, yes it was. Planes lasted a long time if you looked after them. Think of all the Dakotas still doing a day's work in various parts of the world. And even Concorde was getting pretty long in the tooth, and there was no talk of scrapping it yet awhile. Not that he'd heard of anyway.

And now the Catalina was very low indeed, and a moment later it had touched the surface of that dead calm sea and the water was taking the way off it as surely as any brake.

'It is,' Devon said. 'It really and truly is.'

'What is it?'

'A Catalina. I never dreamed of seeing one, never. But what on earth is it doing here?'

He could not be absolutely sure that this plane was an amphibian, because not all Catalinas had been equipped with the retractable tricycle undercarriage, but he believed it likely; it made the aircraft so much more versatile.

In answer to his question Jessica said in her matter of fact way: 'It's coming into the cove, that's what it's doing.'

And he could see that it was. The propellers were still turning and the plane was taxiing into the inlet. A little later it had come to a stop and a man was out on the hull dropping a small anchor from the bows.

'Have you seen it before?' Devon asked.

'Yes. But I've never watched it landing.'

'So it comes pretty often?'

'I'd say so.'

'Do you know where it comes from?'

'No, I don't.'

'Does Duke know about it?'

'Oh yes, he knows.'

'And does he know where it comes from?'

'I can't say. I've never asked him. If it bothers you so much you'd better ask him yourself.'

'Maybe I will.'

'Why are you so interested in it anyway?' she asked. 'It's got nothing to do with you, has it?'

'Maybe not. But it seems odd. There's something about this I don't quite understand.'

'And that worries you?'

'No, it doesn't worry me. It just intrigues me, that's all. I'd like to know more.'

He felt that there was a mystery here. Why would an ancient flying boat make what was apparently a fairly regular flight to this secluded cove? Surely it was not a passenger service; that would be too improbable to credit. So what was the alternative? Cargo? Possibly. But what kind of cargo?

He asked the question of himself, and being a police officer by profession he was just naturally suspicious of anything out of the ordinary, and the thought came into his mind that he was witnessing in this secluded spot some operation that was not exactly legal. Like a bit of smuggling, for instance. Though what could be worth smuggling into St Joseph, where the population was so small? Narcotics? Hardly likely, seeing how limited the market must be. The exercise would not have been profitable enough to make it worth the bother.

He saw now that a boat had set out from the jetty and was approaching the Catalina. The distance was a short one, and in a little while the boat was alongside the aircraft. A minute or two passed, and then it looked as though some packages were being passed across from one boat to the other. From the position on the hillside where he and Jessica were situated it was impossible for Devon to see what kind of packages they were, and indeed the men doing the handling seemed no bigger than animated toys. But what he could see was enough to strengthen his belief that this was a clandestine operation and that the packages were indeed some description of contraband.

'What I really need,' he said, 'is a pair of binoculars. I'd get a clearer picture then.'

'I don't see why you want a clearer picture,' Jessica said. 'What good would it do?'

'I'd like to know what's in those parcels.'

'Why?'

'It could be contraband.'

'You're just imagining things. It's probably all completely innocent. You've no reason at all for thinking it's not. And besides, you're not even on duty.'

'A police officer can never be entirely off duty,' Devon said. 'But you may be right. Maybe I'm being just a bit too suspicious.'

'Now you're talking sense. We're supposed to be enjoying ourselves, remember? Forget that silly old plane. What can you do about it anyway?'

He saw that the boat was leaving the Catalina and heading back to the jetty. And then he noticed something else as well. Three mules were being led down the gully by another man. He took them to the jetty, and when the boat arrived the packages in it were taken out and loaded on to the mules. When they had all been transferred the mules were led back up the gully and Devon lost sight of them. The whole operation had taken less than half an hour.

He wondered whether the Catalina would immediately take off again on the return flight to wherever it had come from. But it did not. So perhaps it was going to remain in the cove for the night. Possibly it would need to take on more fuel, though at present there was no sign of such an operation taking place. And with its long range it might not need refuelling.

'Satisfied now?' Jessica asked.

He was not satisfied, and he would not be until he had found out what kind of goods were in those packages that the Catalina had brought. If only he had known where the plane had come from it might have helped. But about that he could only guess, and any guesses he made might be way off the mark.

But he did not tell her any of this, because it seemed to bother her that he should take so much interest in something that to her was obviously of no significance. Perhaps she was jealous of anything that might divert his attention when it should have been devoted entirely to her on this particular day. As she had said, they were supposed to be enjoying themselves.

'Okay, Jess,' he said. 'If you're ready to go, I am.'

Chapter Ten

HOLT

'Sure,' Morton said, 'I know about that old flying boat. Drops in here now and then.'

'Know where it comes from?' Devon asked.

He had tackled Morton on the subject at the first opportunity, but the detective sergeant appeared to be quite unconcerned.

'No, I don't.'

'Aren't you interested?'

It seemed unbelievable to Devon that Morton should not have made himself acquainted with everything concerning those Catalina flights. Could it be that he was lying? Was he feigning ignorance in order not to become involved? But if so, for what reason? It just did not make sense.

'Why should I be interested?' Morton asked.

'But if contraband is being smuggled into the country—'

'Hey, hey! Who said anythin' 'bout that?'

'Well, it's a possibility, isn't it?'

'What sorta contraband you talkin' 'bout, Frank?'

'At a guess, I'd say drugs.'

'Oh, man!' Morton said. 'You're way over the top. Ain't no drug problem on this island.'

'Is that a fact?'

'Sure is.'

Devon did not believe it, but he refrained from saying so.

He said: 'I saw some stuff being brought ashore from the Catalina in Salt Cove.'

'Don't prove it was anythin' illegal.'

'It looked highly suspicious to me. Don't you think it ought to be investigated?'

Morton gave a slow shake of the head. 'Frank, my man, you tryin' too hard. Let me give you a word of advice. While you're here don't go ferretin' into anythin' you don't have to. Jus' leave it be. Ignore it.'

'Is that what you do?'

'I do my job,' Morton said. 'And I keep my nose clean.'

'Maybe I should tell Horler about it.'

Morton shrugged. 'You feel like it, you go tell him. See where it gets you.'

Detective Inspector Christian Horler looked gloomy when Devon told him. Since this was his normal expression, there was nothing to be deduced from it.

'You sure that's what you saw?'

'Yes.'

'And you think it was a smuggling operation?'

'That's what it looked like to me.'

Horler seemed to be turning the matter over in his mind for a few moments. Then he said: 'This looks like one for the super. Let's go see the man.'

Detective Superintendent Calthorpe Christy was in his office. After Horler had informed him that Devon had some important information to impart he gave a deep sigh and said:

'Well, let's have it. And it'd better be good because I'm a busy man.'

He did not look busy. He was smoking a cigar and there seemed to be nothing on the desk in front of him that was requiring his urgent attention. But perhaps the business was all going on inside his head and he really was hard at work while apparently taking his ease in the armchair which, though large, could scarcely accommodate such a monstrous amount of human flesh.

Thus urged, Devon let him have it. And Christy listened in silence until he had finished his account. Then he drew a copious mouthful of smoke from the cigar, allowed it to drift out again, stared hard at Devon and said:

'So you think we may have a case of smuggling on our hands, do you, sergeant?'

'I don't know, sir. I just think it might bear looking into.'

'And quite right too,' Christy said. 'I agree.'

Devon was pleasantly surprised. He had feared that the superintendent would tell him to forget it, as Morton in effect had. And for that matter, Jessica too. It was gratifying to discover that an officer of Christy's rank was prepared to take the matter seriously.

'So what will you do, sir?'

'I'll get some of my best men on to it straightaway.'

'And I?'

'You?' Christy said.

'What do you wish me to do?'

'Nothing.'

'Nothing, sir? But I thought—'

'You thought you'd be handling it? Sorry. No way. You've done your whack; now it's a matter for my men to take it in hand and carry on from here.'

'But—'

Christy held up a fat hand. 'No buts. I've made my decision and that's final. Now get back to your duties.'

'What did he say?' Morton asked.

'He said he'd put his best men on the case.'

Morton grinned. 'So that lets you and me out of it.'

'Apparently.'

'He didn't say who those best men were?'

'No. But he did seem impressed by the need for prompt action to be taken.'

'He won't do a thing,' Morton said.

Devon glanced at him sharply. 'Why do you say that?'

'I know him, that's why. He's a lazy bastard like I told you before. He never starts anything if he ain't forced to. He'll make a note of what you told him – in his head – and then he'll forget it.'

'But he seemed so impressed.'

'Seemed is the right word. But look at it this way. That flying boat has been coming to this island for who knows how long, and he's never taken a bit of notice before. So why would he start now just because some smart Alick copper from London walks in and tells him to get up off his fat arse and do something about it?'

Devon had to admit that there might be truth in what Morton was saying, and he felt the wind had been rather taken out of his sails. He no longer believed that Christy would take the matter in hand. He had just been fobbed off with that talk of the best men being put on the job; it had all been moonshine. It was galling, but he had to face the fact.

But was indolence the true reason why Christy would take no action? He remembered how quickly the investigation into the death of the man found on the north beach had been shelved. Could there be any connection? He could see none. But the thought, having once come into his mind unbidden, stayed there like a burr, nagging.

It was in the evening two days later when a man stopped him just where he turned on to the dirt road that would take him the last fifty yards or so to his chalet. In the glare of the headlamps he could see the man with a hand raised, and slightly beyond him the car that had apparently brought him there.

Devon halted the Escort, and the man came to the window. He was a white, and looking at him Devon's immediate impression was of a tough self-assured character, maybe a shade above average height, with a lean tanned face and hair like old frayed rope.

'Mr Devon, I believe,' he said.

'You believe right,' Devon replied; and it came to him then that he had seen this man before; only then he had had a hat on covering most of the tow and had been walking away from the Arthurton morgue after looking at the body from the beach. Hearing him speak, it was easy to guess that he was an American. 'What can I do for you?'

'Now that,' the man said, 'is a good question. First I'd rate it as a favour if you'd spare me a few minutes of your time.'

'For what purpose?'

'Talk. You mind if I get in the car?'

'Help yourself,' Devon said. He was interested to hear what the American had to say.

The man walked round to the other side of the car and got in and closed the door behind him.

'Might be best,' he said, 'if you switched the lights off.'

'Why?'

'Don't want to make ourselves conspicuous, do we? Never kmow who may be looking.'

'You're being very cautious.'

'Betcher life I am. And with good reason.'

Devon switched off the lights. He had already killed the

engine. The thought now crossed his mind that the man could easily haul out a knife and stab him in the side, but it seemed unlikely and he did not let the possibility bother him.

'Name's Holt,' the man said. 'Adam Holt. You've seen me before, haven't you?'

'That's true. At the morgue, and then again at The Buccaneer. You went to look at the body that was found on the north beach. Why?'

'To check if it was the guy I guessed it could be.'

'But it wasn't.'

'Wrong,' Holt said. 'It was.'

'You told the attendant you didn't recognize him.'

'Sure I did. Seemed best.'

'I'm a bit fogged,' Devon said. 'Why are you telling me this?'

'Because I think I can trust you, and I could use some help, that's for sure.'

'Help! From me! But you know nothing about me.'

'Wrong again. When I saw you with that black detective I got to wondering what was going on. Seemed pretty damn odd. No white officers in the Arthurton police, so what in hell were you doing there? I make some enquiries; very discreet inquiries, you understand. And what I hear is you're a London cop over here on some kind of exchange deal. Just temporary. That right?'

Devon saw no point in denying the fact. 'It is.'

'So that's why I'm putting myself out on a limb. I wouldn't trust any of those Arthurton cops, but I figure that you being new here, you won't have had time to be corrupted.'

'You think the others are?'

'Maybe not all. But how in hell do you pick the good guys from the bad?'

'I think before we go any further,' Devon said, 'you'd better tell me who that dead man was.'

'Name of Daniel O'Hara. United States Anti-Narcotics agent. He was my buddie. He must've got too close and they got him. Bastards put a bullet through his brain, stripped him naked and left him for somebody to find.'

'Why dump the body on that beach?'

'A warning.'

'To you?'

'Sure. Who else? Go away or you could be the next. That was the message.'

So he had been right about that. It was what he had suggested to Horler, and the suggestion had not gone down too well.

'And now they're on to you too?'

'No. If they were I wouldn't be here talking to you right now. I'd be dead.'

'But if they don't know about you, why the warning?'

'My guess is they're acting on the assumption that Dan wouldn't have been working alone, and it's got them worried.'

He had not yet mentioned who 'they' were, and Devon had not asked. He could have made a rough guess and it might have been somewhere near the mark.

He said: 'The investigation into the killing of your man was called off pretty quickly.'

'Figures,' Holt said.

'You think it's significant?'

'Don't you?'

'I don't know.'

He hardly knew what to think. Holt was opening up a real can of worms, and he wondered just who he could trust. And of course the big question was: could he trust Holt? But what motive could there be for the man to lie?

Then Holt said: 'Have you seen the Catalina?'

'So you know about that?'

'I know about it, and I see you do too.'

'Do you know where it comes from?'

'Can't be certain, but my guess is Colombia.'

'Ah!' Devon said. And it seemed to him that some pieces in a jigsaw puzzle were fitting together. 'Carrying what?'

'Cocaine. What else? Can't you see how an amphibian would be just the thing for this business? It could pick up a load from some landing strip in the interior of the country and come down on the water at this end of the flight.'

'Are you sure it is the amphibious version?'

'Oh yes. I've had a look at it through binoculars. I've seen the wheels.'

'But,' Devon said, 'there's something I still don't understand. Why bring the stuff to a place like this? The market couldn't possibly be big enough to make the operation worthwhile.'

'It sure wouldn't. But this is only a staging post. What happens is this: the coke is stashed in some place near Salt Cove and picked up by boats, even maybe small ships anchored offshore. From here it could go to the States or Europe. It's a helluva smart arrangement, wouldn't you say?'

'Yes, I would.'

'Question is: where are they storing it?'

'You don't know?'

'Not yet. I'm still looking. And that's where I thought you might help.'

Devon was not enthusiastic. He was not at all sure he wanted to be drawn into some clandestine operation instigated by an American secret agent whom he knew so little about.

He said warily: 'I'm not sure I can. I'm attached to the Arthurton police for the present. And I take it that what you're suggesting would be done without their approval.'

'Right in one. There's no way I'd be working with that lot; no way at all. No, sir.'

'That's what I thought. Now correct me if I'm wrong, but I get the impression that you're not really supposed to be on this island at all.'

'Well,' Holt said, 'let's just say I didn't come in through the regular gate. Fact is, me and Dan were put ashore from a boat one dark night. That way you get more freedom of action.'

'Including the freedom to get a bullet in the napper.'

'The rub of the green. It's a risk we all have to take in this kinda business.'

'And one you're inviting me to take?'

'You can always say no.'

'That's true.'

And he knew it was what he ought to say. It was no part of his contract to go lending a hand to a secret agent who was not even legally on the island. It could spell trouble for him, big trouble. And yet he felt drawn to it. The risk was there without a doubt, but even that had a certain attraction.

He said: 'They use mules to carry the packages away. Did you know that?'

'No,' Holt said, 'I didn't. I've never seen the stuff being unloaded. Mules, huh? That's interesting. If we could find where they go it would answer our question.'

Devon noticed that he was using the plural pronoun, as though already counting on an acceptance.

He said: 'There's something else you ought to know. There's a very rich Colombian living here.'

'Is that a fact? You know him?'

'I've met him. My partner and I paid a visit to his house a few days ago. There'd been a garbled telephone call, sounded like somebody was getting killed. So we went along. Place is all walled in, with an armed guard on the gate. House is like a palace. Man's name is Jorge Ramirez. Handsome bastard.'

'So who was being killed?'

'Nobody, according to him. Our guess was that he was giving his wife a beating and the housekeeper got scared and called the police. When we got there the wife, Dolores, was in a bikini by the swimming-pool reading a book. She denied being beaten, but I think she had a black eye.'

'You think?'

'She was wearing dark glasses. Ramirez said the housekeeper was crazy, but I doubt it. He looked to me like a man very capable of giving his wife a black eye, and more besides if he felt like it.'

'And you think he could be connected with the cocaine imports?'

'I don't know. It seems possible. You'd hardly expect a Colombian to be living here if he didn't have some special interest in the place, would you?'

'No,' Holt said. 'And I guess they might need an agent on the island to arrange things at this end. Could be Dan O'Hara got on to him and paid the price.'

'At first I thought the man might have been using this as a refuge from enemies he'd made in his own country. But this seems just as probable.'

'Could be both. Working for one lot and hiding from another. They're at one another's throats all the time in that goddam country.'

'So what exactly are you asking me to do?' Devon asked.

'Keep your eyes and ears open. Any information you can get hold of and you think might be useful, I'd be glad to hear it. You've made a start as it is. I didn't know about that Ramirez guy.'

'We still don't know for certain he's mixed up in the drug trade.'

'No, but it all points that way. I'd better go now. I hope I can trust you not to talk about this to anyone.'

'You don't want me to consult my partner, Duke Morton?'

'Not even him. You confide in one guy and it doesn't stop there; it gets around.'

'You took the risk in confiding in me,' Devon said.

'I know. Maybe it was a fool thing to do. But hell, you gotta chance your arm sometimes. And I sure do need all the help I can get.'

He had his hand on the door catch and was about to open it.

'How do I get in touch with you?' Devon asked.

'You don't. I'll be in touch with you.'

'So you're not going to tell me where you're hanging out?'

'No. Best you don't know.'

'So you still don't really trust me?'

'It's not a matter of trust. It's policy.'

He opened the door and got out.

'Mind how you go,' Devon said.

Holt gave a laugh that was like a bark. 'It's what I do. All the time. That's the way I've managed to stay alive. So far.'

Chapter Eleven

TREASURE

Jessica was waiting for him when he went in. She greeted him with a hug and a kiss. For him she made every homecoming an event to be looked forward to with pleasure. And all the evidence seemed to indicate that she regarded it with equal delight. They had not yet been living together long enough for any of the gilt to be rubbed off the gingerbread. Her eyes still lighted up when she saw him, and his heart gave a kick when she swam into his line of sight. It might not last, but while it did it was great, just great.

'Had a good day, Frank?'

'So, so.'

'Anything exciting happened?'

'Nothing out of the ordinary.'

And perhaps that was not entirely the truth. There had been that encounter with Adam Holt. That had certainly been no ordinary meeting. But he had no intention of telling her about that. Because if he told her, he knew it would not be long before

Ida heard about it, and then Duke, and it would not stop there. So he kept it to himself as Holt had asked him to do. And he wondered just what he was letting himself in for if he went along with Holt. Some pretty sticky business indeed, perhaps; because they would be dealing with the kind of people who would stop at nothing to protect their interests. The bastards had already murdered Holt's partner, and that was surely warning enough to avoid treading on their toes.

Well, he could still pull out; he had committed himself to nothing, and all he had to do when next Holt got in touch with him was to say he had thought things over and was no longer interested in sticking his neck out. But that would have been a lie, for he was still interested, very much so; and he knew in his heart that when the time came he would not pull out. It might be madness to press ahead when he knew the risks he would be taking for no really compelling reason, since the business was all outside his assignment; but if so then he was mad and there was an end of it. Or maybe just the start; for one thing would surely lead to another, and no one could tell what the final outcome would be.

'Frank darling,' Jessica said, 'you're looking very thoughtful. Is there something on your mind?'

'No,' he said. 'Nothing. Except you. These days you're always on my mind. I think of nothing else.'

'That's nice,' she said. 'That really is nice. Because there's nowhere in the world I'd rather be.' And then she smiled and added: 'Except in your arms of course.'

*

Two days passed, and it was all routine work. There had been a break-in at one of the big houses, and they went along to investigate. The place was no fortress like Ramirez's, and the house was on a more modest scale. The owner was a native of St Joseph and had a shop in the best part of Arthurton. It was apparently doing pretty well for Mr McBride, a stout middle-aged man who was most indignant at being robbed.

'You work hard to make a success of life. You buy some nice things to make your home look real good. And what happens? Some good-for-nothing thief comes along and takes them.'

Mrs McBride, who was built on a similar generous scale to that of her husband, backed him up.

'It's not fair. It breaks your heart.'

It appeared that the burglary had taken place during the night, and no one in the house had heard a sound. The French windows, which opened on to a patio, had been forced, and the intruders had got in by that way. They had taken only things that were easily portable: a radio, a video, a microwave oven, some silverware, a coffee-maker and various other items, including some valuable Persian rugs. They had made a mess of the place too, which seemed to upset Mrs McBride as much as the material loss.

Devon could sympathize with her. It was not at all nice having your house burgled and vandalised. Some people never got over the shock.

Morton took notes, assured the McBrides that everything possible would be done to catch the culprits and left the fingerprint man to do his work on the French windows and other surfaces.

'So what's the next move?' Devon asked as they drove away.

'The next move,' Morton said, 'is to pay a call on the usual suspects.'

The usual suspects were in shanty town. Morton seemed to have an instinct for such things and he went straight to the right place. The thieves were a couple of brothers living in an old furniture van. They were so unprofessional that they had not yet cached the loot or sold it to a fence. It was all there in the van. They were only petty criminals and they made no resistance when Morton showed his gun.

'The McBrides will be pleased,' Devon said. 'Is it always as easy as this?'

'Not likely. I had a hunch and we just struck lucky. Another time you could nose around all over the place and never get a sniff of a lead.'

'Like with the body on the beach?'

'Now that,' Morton said, 'was a different kinda business altogether. No good lookin' in shanty town for the guys that did that job.'

He was right about that, Devon thought. He could have told Morton of a more likely place to look, and it was where both of them had recently gone on quite a different matter. But he held his peace.

*

Later that day Adam Holt turned up again. Same time. Same spot. Devon held the car door open for him and he slipped into the passenger seat.

'You still with me, Frank?' he asked.

'I'm right beside you,' Devon said.

'Physically, yes. For the moment. But you know that's not what I meant.'

'What have you got in mind?'

'I think we should take a look for that place where they're stashing the drugs.'

'We don't yet know they are drugs.'

'Well, that's as may be. But me, I'd lay a thousand to one in dollars that they are.'

'And I wouldn't take you even at those odds.'

'So I'll say it again. Are you with me?'

'When are you proposing to make the search?'

'Tonight. There'll be a moon. It'll help.'

'What time?'

'Pick you up at ten. How does that sound?'

It sounded to Devon like the recipe for an argument with Jessica. She would want to know where he was going and why. So he would just have to fob her off. Fortunately, they had arranged nothing in particular for that evening.

'Okay,' he said.

'Good man. We'll go in my car. No need to take yours. Do you carry a gun?'

'No.'

'Pity,' Holt said. 'But maybe there'll be no need.'

Devon hoped there would not.

Jessica was no more pleased than he had expected her to be.

'You're doing what?'

He repeated what he had already said. 'I'm going out.'

'At ten?'

'At ten.'

'Why?'

'There's a job I have to do.'

'With Duke?'

'No, not with Duke. Alone.'

'Does Duke know about this?'

'No.'

'I don't understand,' she said. 'If it's police work why doesn't he know and why isn't he going with you?'

'I can't explain it right now. You'll just have to accept my word that it's necessary.'

'When will you be back?'

'I don't know. But don't wait up for me, because it could be rather late.'

She gave him a shrewd searching look. 'You're doing something you ought not to, aren't you? Something unofficial.'

'I'm doing what I have to do,' he said.

It did not satisfy her.

'Oh God!' she said. 'I hope you're not proposing to do something really crazy.'

'Like what, for instance?'

'Like running into danger. Like risking your life over some hare-brained investigation of your own.' And then the answer seemed to hit her and she said: 'It's to do with that flying boat, isn't it? You've still got that on your mind. You can't leave it alone.'

'You're imagining things,' Devon said.

'So tell me I'm wrong.'

'You're wrong,' he said.

And it occurred to him that this was the first time he had told her a downright lie.

He was not happy about that.

Holt was there dead on time. Devon got into the car, which was a hired Nissan, and they set off.

'So you didn't decide to pull out after all,' Holt said.

'No, I hadn't sense enough.'

'Sounds like it still bothers you.'

'To be perfectly honest, it does. But I'm committed now and I'll go through with it.'

'But you don't feel driven to it for any particular compelling reason?'

'No. Do you?'

'Bet your sweet life, I do.'

'So what's the reason? Tell me.'

Holt hesitated for a few moments before apparently deciding that he might as well give the whole story. 'Okay then, I'll tell you. I had a brother. He got hooked on the stuff. Speed, acid, crack, big H. You name it, he used it. Killed him in the end. Took time. I watched him breaking up. He got into crime to make money to feed the habit. He was a decent kid before the pushers got to him; after that he went down and down. Nothing I could do; he wouldn't listen to me. There came a time he was like a stranger. Gaunt. Arms like pin-cushions. You ever have anybody close to you go down that road, Frank?'

'Can't say I have,' Devon said. But he could see now why Holt was so committed. With him it was a personal thing. The loss of a well-loved brother might have made him fanatical about what he was doing. And really the last thing that he, Devon, wanted on his hands was a fanatic as a partner. You could never be certain what crazy action a man like that might take. And involve you in it.

And then, as if to lend strength to this misgiving, Holt said: 'I'd like to kill every last one of the sons-a-bitches in that traffic. I know it's not possible, but I may get a few of 'em before I'm finished with the job.'

Devon wondered whether those few included certain people on the island of St Joseph. And he feared it did.

Holt said: 'Of course I don't kid myself that even if I put a stop to some of the junk leaking into the States by way of this rathole it'll be more than a drop in the bucket. But hell, you gotta do what you can. And if only for Dan O'Hara's sake I owe these bastards something.'

He did not drive back into town, but took the coast road on the south side, which was a shorter route to Salt Cove than the journey via Logan's Bay. He had done some reconnaissance in daylight and he knew a place where they could leave the car well hidden from the road and then go the rest of the way on foot. They had brought torches, and Devon knew that Holt was armed, though he himself was not. He hoped there would be no shooting, but felt no confidence that there would not be. Holt might not be trigger-happy, but he was obviously not a man to be squeamish about using the gun if he felt it at all necessary.

After about ten minutes of scrambling over some pretty rough and fairly steeply rising ground, where Devon allowed Holt to lead the way, they found themselves at a point overlooking Salt Cove. It was not the place from which he and Jessica had observed the Catalina coming in, but was on the seaward side of the road and rather further to the south. At this point they were considerably closer to the cove and not very far from the head of the gully down which on that previous occasion Devon had seen the mules descending to pick up the packages that had been ferried ashore from the flying boat.

'No Catalina tonight,' he said.

In the moonlight it would certainly have been visible if it had been there. There was a light breeze cooling the air and rippling the water of the inlet, but as far as could be observed there was no activity whatever down there.

'I'd give something to know the flight schedule,' Holt said.

'At a guess I'd say it's irregular, but even that's not certain. Those guys running this operation don't seem much concerned about the risk element. Maybe they know there ain't one.'

Devon did not ask him to elaborate on that remark; he had no difficulty in working things out for himself. The implication was disturbing but perhaps not entirely unjustified. Unfortunately.

The jetty was in the shadow of the cliff, but it was just possible to make out the shape of a bigger boat than any that had been there on the other occasion. It could have been a cabin cruiser, and indeed there was a glimmer of light showing, which was probably coming from inside the superstructure. He drew Holt's attention to it.

'That one wasn't here last time I saw the place. Wonder where it came from.'

'I could make a guess,' Holt said. 'Boat that size could make quite a long sea voyage. Probably a fast mover too. What d'you say?'

'I'd say you're right.'

'Those guys in that boat,' Holt said, 'I'd like to go down there and put some questions to them.'

'I doubt whether you'd get any civil answers.'

And of course it was not on. Try that and the answer might well be a bullet in the brainbox. And what good would that do for the cause of law and order?

'Maybe I should just go in there with the gun. Shoot them and ask questions after.'

'Now that,' Devon said, 'you really can leave me out of.'

Holt gave a low chuckle. 'Just a thought.'

'Keep it at that.'

'Okay. So now I guess we better start hunting for that place where they store the junk.'

'Why don't we start at the top of the gully and work our way back from there?'

'Makes sense,' Holt said. 'Let's go.'

They moved back from the edge of the cliff and made their way to the left, not using the torches for fear of attracting attention to themselves, but relying on the moonlight to show the way. The ground was uneven and they had to walk carefully to avoid the pitfalls lying in wait for the unwary. But the vegetation was sparse in this part and they soon reached the gully where it emerged at the top of its ascent from the beach. Here it was possible to detect a rough track leading away from the cove and descending a gentle slope.

There was no need for any debate. It was obvious that this was the way the mules must have gone, and without hesitation they set off along the beaten track, Holt in the lead and Devon close behind.

Very soon the trail plunged into a kind of arboreal tunnel formed by the branches of trees meeting overhead. Here the moonlight was almost completely shut out, but still they refrained from using the torches, and the wisdom of this was proved a minute or two later when they heard men's voices just ahead.

Holt stopped and said in a low voice: 'I think we better get off the trail. If I'm not much mistaken those guys are heading this way.'

Devon agreed, and they plunged into the dark greenery on one side. A few yards into this cover they turned and looked back. They had moved away only just in time, for the voices had grown louder and a moment or two later it was possible to tell that there were two men having an argument over something. They reached the spot where Devon and Holt had been standing shortly before and a wavering light which might have been coming from a lantern showed through the leaves. There were enough gaps also to reveal that the man with the lantern was walking slightly ahead of the other one, who was leading a string of three mules, almost certainly those which Devon had seen on a previous occasion.

The mules were carrying packs, and it took very little brilliance of mind to deduce that these burdens were destined to be put on board the cabin cruiser waiting at the jetty.

Soon this little baggage train had passed on its way and the lantern light had vanished. The men's voices faded in the distance and the two searchers came out of hiding.

Holt was cursing. Somehow the sight of those packages going past him almost within touching distance seemed to have infuriated him.

'Under our very noses, and we let them go.'

'What else could we have done?'

'I could have shot the bastards, that's what.'

'And a hell of a lot of use that would have been. Two dead

black mule drivers wouldn't make tuppence worth of difference to the junk trade.'

'I know, I know. But it sure is galling. Makes a guy mad.'

'Well, how about the mad guy hitting the trail again so we can do some more of what we were doing before the interruption.'

'Okay. Let's go.'

Back on the trail it was obvious to both men that they had only to follow it in the direction from which the mules had come. This must inevitably lead them to the place where the packages had been stored. The only way they could go wrong was by wandering off the trail; but this had become so well marked by the hoofs of the mules on what were almost certainly frequent journeys that even where the moonlight failed to penetrate there was no difficulty in keeping to the beaten track. There were a few meanderings but the way was steadily downhill until finally they came to a shallow bowl.

'Eureka!' Holt exclaimed.

It was the right word. For they had certainly found something, and all the odds were on its being what they had been looking for. Holt might have shouted in triumph, but it would have been folly to do so, since there was no telling who might be within earshot. So he uttered the word only softly, but with a note of exultation, as they stopped for a moment on the rim of the bowl and stared at what they had discovered.

Yet even now it could not be taken for granted that this was indeed what they had been searching for, though it certainly appeared so probable as to leave little room for doubt.

'Seek and ye shall find,' Devon said. 'But what have we found? That is the question.'

'So let's go see.'

They walked towards it over some bare rough ground, and in the moonlight it was revealed as a long low building with a roof that might have been corrugated iron. There was no light showing from it and there was no sign of habitation in any other part of the hollow, which was hardly big enough to accommodate much more than this one rather unimpressive structure.

When they came to it they could tell that it was no more than a shed with rough wooden walls and a door at one end. They walked all round it and discovered that there were two windows on each side. Holt shone his torch on one of these windows, but the glass was so dirty it was impossible to make out what was inside.

'We'll have to go in,' he said.

Devon was in agreement with that. They had found what was with scarcely a shadow of doubt the storehouse from which the packs on the mules had come, but they could not yet be sure of what was in them.

They went back to the door. It was padlocked.

'Who in hell did they think would break in?' Holt said.

'People like us perhaps,' Devon suggested.

'I could maybe shoot the goddam lock off.'

'And bring them running?'

'Not a good idea, huh?'

'Not good at all.'

They examined one of the windows. It was of the casement type, fastened on the inside.

'No problem,' Holt said.

He broke one of the panes of glass with the butt of his pistol, reached inside and released the catch. It was stiff and rusty, apparently not having been touched for some time; under the pressure of his hand it moved with a screeching noise which sounded loud to Devon's ears but could have been heard only by someone standing very near.

Holt pulled the window open, and this protested noisily also. He climbed over the sill and Devon followed. There was a fusty odour in the shed, and it was warm, having retained much of the heat of the day in that confined space. The torches of the two intruders revealed large stacks of polythene bags, with alleyways between the stacks.

'Well now,' Holt said. 'What have we here?'

He put down his torch, took a clasp-knife from his pocket, opened it, and with Devon providing light for the operation, made a slit in one of the bags. Some white powder trickled out.

'Bingo!'

He moistened the end of his right index finger and dipped it in the powder. With the tip of his tongue he tasted the grains adhering to the finger and spat them out.

'It's the real McCoy,' he said.

'Cocaine?'

'Sure thing.'

He picked up his torch again and sent the beam wandering

round the shed, revealing stack after stack of the polythene bags.

'My, oh my! There's a fortune here. I couldn't even begin to guess how many millions of dollars this lot would be worth on the streets of New York or Los Angeles.'

'Not to mention London, Paris and Amsterdam,' Devon said. 'The mind, as they say, boggles.'

For a while they both stood in silence, as if awed by the sight of that vast treasure, not of jewels or gold, but of a plain white powder that had started life as the leaves of an insignificant shrub in the shadow of the lofty Andes.

They were still lost in this silent contemplation when they heard a sound that could only have been made by the men returning with the mules, perhaps for another load.

Chapter Twelve

SQUEEZED OUT

They switched off the torches. A glimmer of moonlight revealed the window by which they had come in.

'Time to leave,' Holt said.

He moved to the window and cautiously put his head out; then quickly withdrew it.

'Did you see them?' Devon asked.

'Sure. Coming this way.'

'Awkward.'

'You said it.'

Holt waited a few moments and then took another peep out of the window. This time he did not withdraw his head so quickly. When he did so he was able to report that the men and the mules were no longer in view.

'They must be round the corner. I guess this is where we make our exit.'

He wasted no more time and was quickly through the open window. Devon soon joined him outside, and they paused with their backs hard up against the wall of the shed. They could hear the two mule drivers carrying on a conversation in high-pitched voices. They still seemed to be arguing about something. It could have been a habit with them.

'I wonder whether they're armed,' Devon said.

'Good question.'

Holt had his own pistol in his hand, and Devon just hoped he would have no occasion to use it. When guns were used people had a way of getting killed.

One of the mule drivers shouted suddenly: 'Well, unlock the door, can't you? What you waitin' for?'

The other one mumbled something in answer that Devon failed to catch; but the gist immediately became apparent when the first one cried out in obvious exasperation:

'You dropped the key! Well, pick it up, man, pick it up.'

'Can't find it. Bring the light.'

There was some grumbling from the man with the lantern, but apparently he did what was requested, and a moment later there was a shout.

'There it is. Now open up. You wanna be here all night?'

Holt whispered: 'Maybe they'll both go inside. Then we'll make tracks.'

'Why not try a detour?' Devon suggested.

But Holt was not in favour. 'Get ourselves in that jungle and we could lose our bearings and wander around for God knows how long. Best go back up the trail, the way we came.'

A moment later they heard the screech of unoiled hinges as

the door of the shed was opened. Holt crept up to the end of the wall and peered round the corner. He made a beckoning signal with his finger and hissed:

'Now!'

Immediately he himself was off like a hare, with Devon close at his heels. The mules came into view, standing in a dejected-looking group to the right of the shed door, which was now open. There was no sign of the two drivers, who must have been inside.

They had almost reached the place where the trail came out of the trees at the edge of the bowl when Devon heard a shout. Glancing over his shoulder, he could see that one of the blacks had come out of the hut and had spotted the intruders in the moonlight. The question of whether or not the mule-drivers were armed was now answered in a most unwelcome manner; at least regarding one of them. Devon saw this man go into a gun-fighter's crouch, and then there was the crack of a pistol and something whistled past his ear, too close for comfort.

'Sonuvabitch!' Holt snarled.

He turned back and took quick aim at the shooter with his own weapon, firing almost instantly. It was either a lucky shot or he was an expert with a pistol, for the mule-driver gave a cry and dropped his gun. He had been winged for certain, and now the other man was coming out of the hut to see what was going on.

Holt and Devon waited no longer but set off up the trail, running. They were some three-quarters of the way back to the cliff when they almost collided with someone hurrying in the opposite direction. It was another black man. He had a torch and he came to a sudden stop as the light from it revealed them to him. They had stopped also, and for a moment no one spoke. Then the man said:

'What you doin'? Who in hell are you?'

Holt answered innocently: 'Just two people out for a stroll. And never mind who we are. It's none of your business.'

As he was speaking he had been moving closer to the other man, who seemed confused. Holt put paid to the confusion by taking a last quick step towards him and aiming a shrewd blow at his head with the pistol in his hand. The man went down and did not get up or make any attempt to do so. He was out for the count.

They left him there and reached the cliff-top without further incident. A short while later they were on the road and heading towards the place where the car had been left.

'So now we know,' Holt said.

The night's work was finished and soon they were leaving Salt Cove well behind them. Devon felt that it had all been very satisfactory, though the shooting had been regrettable.

'Yes,' he said, 'now we know. We've had the answer to one question, but now there's another. What do we do next?'

'That's an easy one to answer,' Holt said. 'Next we figure out a way to destroy that dump. And the Catalina too, if possible.'

Devon had grave doubts regarding this proposal, in which it was evident that Holt was including him. It seemed that what the American had in mind was some crazy scheme of pretty large scale mayhem, and he was not at all sure he wished to be a part of it. In fact he was damned certain he did not.

'I've got a better idea.'

Holt glanced at him. 'Yeah? Let's have it.'

'It seems to me the best thing would be if I reported what we've discovered to the Arthurton police.'

'Jesus Christ!' Holt said. 'Are you out of your mind?'

'Certainly not. After all, I'm a police officer myself. It's my duty to pass on this information to higher authority. Then they can handle the situation in whatever way they think fit.'

'My, oh my! I do believe you're serious.'

'Of course I'm serious. Why wouldn't I be?'

'Are you telling me you trust those guys?'

'You don't?'

'You said it, Frank.'

They were silent for a while, Holt concentrating on his driving and Devon thinking about that little matter of trust. Did he really trust those guys, as Holt had called them? That was a difficult question to answer. Would he have been willing to put his life in the hands of Detective Superintendent Calthorpe Christy for example? The answer to that had to be in the negative. But that was not really the question. The question was could Christy be trusted to act on the information he was proposing to take to him? And here again the answer was no. Not entirely.

But Christy was not the ultimate authority; there were those superior to him who could be appealed to if the fat man gave no satisfaction. And in this matter he would not hesitate to go over Christy's head, whatever the consequences of so doing might be.

'Well,' Holt said at last, 'if you really are set on doing what you said, I hope you'll promise me one thing.'

'What's that?'

'That you'll keep my name out of it. That you won't mention me at all.'

'You want me to claim I found the dump on my own?'

'That's it.'

Devon thought about it, and came to the conclusion that there was no reason why he should not do this. It might in fact be the best way, since his relationship with Adam Holt would be difficult to explain at all satisfactorily. So he said:

'All right. I'll leave you out.'

Jessica woke when he got into bed. She turned to him drowsily and said:

'So you're back.'

'Yes, I'm back,' he said. And kissed her.

'What time is it?'

'Never mind the time,' Devon said. 'Just go back to sleep. I shouldn't have waked you.'

'What have you been doing?'

'Like I told you. A job.'

'What kind of job?'

'Nothing that would interest you.'

'Which is as much as to say it would interest me very much, but you're not going to tell me a thing about it.'

'Some other time. Not now.'

'I just hope you haven't been doing something that could get you into trouble. Have you?'

'No.'

He could tell that she did not believe him. She was not so easily fooled.

She said: 'I worry about you, Frank. I really do.'

'That's nice,' he said. 'But you have no cause to.'

And he wondered whether that was the truth either.

'I love you, Frank,' she said.

'I love you too, Jess.'

And that at least was no lie.

It was a room at police headquarters in which he had never been before. It was larger than Detective Superintendent Calthorpe Christy's office and was more elaborately furnished. Everything about it bespoke the fact that the man in occupation of this chamber was of a higher rank than the fat man. In fact he was of the highest rank of all.

His name was Magnus McAndrew, and he was Chief of Police and he was sitting at the desk. He was a man of imposing presence; coal-black, broad-shouldered, hard-faced, wearing a pale blue uniform with a lot of gold braid on it and certain decorations which were new to Devon and probably were exclusive to the island of St Joseph.

There was another man sitting in an armchair to the right of the desk. He was lean, his face narrow and heavily pockmarked, hair turning grey, skin brown rather than black, hands like the talons of a bird of prey. He was wearing an immaculate white suit and snakeskin shoes on surprisingly small feet. His eyes were hidden behind dark glasses.

Christy had introduced this individual as Mr Edgar Roylance, Minister for the Interior and Justice in the St Joseph Government.

In the event there had been no need for Devon to insist on passing his piece of information to someone of higher rank than the detective superintendent, for Christy himself had suggested that this would be advisable. Such an important matter, he said, ought only to be handled at the highest level.

Devon had been agreeably surprised at this reaction. He had quite expected Christy to fob him off again with empty promises that the matter would be looked into. He had also been prepared to be severely reprimanded for exceeding his authority, since he had been given direct orders not to take any further part in that investigation. But Christy had not even mentioned this fact; so perhaps he had forgotten, though it seemed unlikely.

And now he was in the presence of these two important personages who were regarding him with interest, not perhaps unmixed with a certain degree of wariness. Or was he merely imagining that?

'So, Sergeant Devon,' McAndrew said, 'it seems you have stumbled upon something of considerable importance. A storehouse, you say, containing a large amount of cocaine. Is that so?'

'Yes, sir.'

'Now let's get this straight. In the first place, can you be sure it was cocaine and not some other perfectly innocent substance?'

'I have no doubt it was cocaine, sir. I slit open one of the bags and a white powder came out. I tasted it. It was the drug all right.'

This was bending the truth a little. It had been Holt's tongue and not his that had done the tasting. But it was all one.

'So you've had experience of that particular drug?'

'Yes. It's not uncommon on the streets of London. A police officer could hardly be ignorant of it.'

'Ah! And so you found this storehouse. When was that?'

'Last night, sir.'

'And where was this?'

'Near Salt Cove.'

'Now something puzzles me, sergeant,' McAndrew said. 'What exactly were you doing out there at that time – which was what would you say, approximately?'

'Between ten and eleven.'

'So at some time between ten and eleven you were wandering about near Salt Cove and you accidentally stumbled on this store. Is that correct?'

'No, sir. It wasn't an accident. I was looking for it.'

'Really? Why?'

'Because on a previous occasion I had seen a Catalina flying boat come into the cove and discharge some packages which were then taken away by mules. This seemed rather strange to me and I suspected a smuggling operation.'

'Did you report this?'

'Yes, sir.'

McAndrew glanced at Christy. 'You knew of this?'

Christy appeared uncomfortable. 'I did, sir, but—'

'What action did you take?'

'Two of my officers made an investigation but were able to find nothing of a suspicious nature.'

'They didn't find any storehouse?'

'No, sir.'

'Perhaps they didn't look closely enough.'

'It may be so, sir.'

Devon would have hazarded a guess that they had not looked at all. He doubted whether Christy had even ordered the search. But he said nothing. He had a feeling that he was not endearing himself very much to the superintendent. Which might have repercussions.

McAndrew treated Christy to a long hard stare, which seemed to cause him more discomfort. Then he said:

'Your men presumably searched in daylight and found nothing. Sergeant Devon went there at night and discovered a storehouse full of cocaine. That doesn't say much for the efficiency of your officers, does it?'

'No, sir.'

The man in the dark glasses spoke for the first time, his tone acid. He said:

'This is a most serious matter. It appears that something nefarious has been going on undetected under our very noses, for how long no one knows, and it takes a British police officer newly posted to this island to discover it within a few days of his arrival. I think we should take a good hard look at our own criminal investigation department, don't you?'

Neither Christy nor McAndrew made any answer to that one. It was evident that both were included in the criticism. Christy was pulling at his lower lip. McAndrew sat stony-faced. Devon could guess that they were boiling inside and would have liked to make an angry retort but did not have the courage to do so.

Edgar Roylance looked at Devon. 'Are we to take it that you were alone in this operation, sergeant?'

'Yes, sir.'

'I commend your zeal. It's not every man who would act so conscientiously, and maybe put himself at risk when he was not under any obligation to do so. Some people might say you were exceeding your authority, that you ought not to have acted as you did without consulting your superiors. That would be splitting hairs in my opinion. I appreciate initiative when I come across it and I judge on results. Let me congratulate you most highly.'

The minister spoke with precision. It put Devon in mind of someone reading from a script.

'Thank you, sir,' he said.

'And now,' Roylance continued, 'it remains for us to deal with this situation without delay.' He turned to McAndrew. 'You will see to that, Magnus?'

'I surely will,' McAndrew said; and he turned a steely glance on Christy, under which that man's pudding of a face seemed to shrink a little. 'At once.'

'What do you wish me to do, sir?' Devon asked.

Roylance gave the faintest of smiles. 'Ah, I see what it is, sergeant. You're still keen to take a hand in this game. I can understand that. You made the discovery and you still feel involved with the operation. Isn't that so?'

'Yes, sir; it is.'

Roylance gave a shake of the head. 'But it's just not on, I'm afraid. This is our affair and it's we who must deal with it. But I can assure you that this time there will be no mistake. Am I right, Magnus? Am I right, superintendent?'

Both men nodded their agreement. There could be no doubt that Edgar Roylance was the one who called the shots.

'It simply remains for me to thank you for the good work you've done, Sergeant Devon. It will not be forgotten; I can assure you of that.'

It was a dismissal. Devon left the room with mixed feelings. The smuggling business was to be taken in hand now; that much was certain. But he felt left out. In a way he had come to regard it as his case, and he would have liked to see it through to a finish. Now, however, he had been squeezed out; the whole operation was out of his hands and had been taken over by others. He felt somehow deflated.

And he wondered what Adam Holt would have to say when he told him of the result of his report.

Chapter Thirteen

WARNING

But for a few days he saw nothing of Holt and therefore could not tell him anything.

He told Morton, again omitting any mention of the part that the American had played in the affair. Morton was not greatly pleased. In fact he was considerably disgruntled.

'What you think you're playing at, Frankie? Goin' off like that on your own account. Why didn't you ask me to go along with you? I'm your partner, ain't I?'

'If I had, would you have gone?'

Morton gave no answer to that.

'Anyway, it paid off, didn't it? Now this smuggling racket will be finally cleaned up.'

'You think so?'

'Of course I do. It's gone right to the top now. And Mr Roylance struck me as being the sort of man who gets things done.'

'Oh, he's that all right,' Morton said. 'He sure does get things done, that Mr Roylance.'

And he grinned suddenly, as though at a private joke.

Devon wondered what he found so amusing, but he did not ask.

And even with Edgar Roylance as the driving force Devon could see no immediate evidence of the wheels of justice revolving in the matter of the drug smuggling operation. Certainly he himself was not being taken into the confidence of those who were running things, and more than ever he had that feeling of being left out of something he himself had started. It galled him a little. They might at least have kept him in the picture.

But then all such thoughts were driven out of his mind by an occurrence which brought home to him in the most brutal of fashions the fact that he was undoubtedly still very intimately involved in the business, whether he had been sidelined or not.

It was two days after his meeting with the top brass. At the end of his tour of duty he took leave of Morton and drove back to the chalet in pleasurable anticipation of being greeted by Jessica as soon as he stepped through the doorway. They would embrace, and she would ask him what sort of day he had had; and then they would have a meal there or go out somewhere to eat. And it would all be so good; the very best part of his life on that beautiful island. Life with her.

But this time it did not work out like that. He went up the steps and opened the door and walked in; but there was no

Jessica smiling enchantingly and moving towards him for the kiss. She was not there, and the chalet was silent.

He called her name; 'Jessica! I'm home.'

There was no answer, and he felt a sudden chill; a shiver running down his spine; a premonition of something bad, of something really bad. And yet there was no good reason for the feeling. She might have stepped out of the chalet for a while and gone somewhere. But her bicycle was outside; he had seen it. And if she had been going into Arthurton she would have used it. And why would she go anywhere at this time of day when she would be expecting him to walk in at any moment? Besides which, the door had not been locked.

So perhaps she was in the bedroom, the one they shared.

Making no sound? Not answering his call? Asleep?

There was one way of finding out, one step to take. And yet he felt a strange reluctance to take it. He stood there, hesitating, and seconds ticked away. The silence was broken only by the low hum of the refrigerator in the kitchen and the faint hissing sound of small waves falling on the beach and retreating.

He forced himself to move. He walked to the door of the bedroom and pushed it open. He went in.

She was lying on the bed where they had left her. Her throat had been cut and the blood had poured out on to the coverlet, staining it with that most precious of dyes.

He felt sick. He had a sense of irretrievable loss. He wanted to rush to the bed, to lift her up, drag her back to life by sheer physical strength or by an effort of will. But he could not. It was not possible. She was gone from him. For a brief while they had been lovers, and now she had departed, never to return.

At last he moved to the bed. There was a slip of paper lying on the body. He took it up and read the words written on it. The message was curt but clear. In block capitals inscribed with a felt-tipped pen he read:

THIS IS A WARNING. KEEP YOUR NOSE OUT. NEXT TIME IT COULD BE YOU.

He began to swear, spitting out the obscenities in a stream of invective. But he stopped abruptly, for of what use was cursing? It would not touch the swine who had done this thing?

And in a sense it was he himself who had killed her. But for him, she would still have been alive. That hard fact could not be denied. And no doubt he would be blamed – by Morton and Ida and the children. He had come to the island and brought this tragedy into their lives.

It was entirely his fault and he knew it. There had been no necessity for him to involve himself in that damned drug smuggling business; he had received no orders to do so; he had even been discouraged from taking any such action. But he had pressed ahead, and he could not plead that he had been driven by any desire for vengeance as Holt was; for him it had been more in the nature of a game which he was eager to win. And what a deadly game it had proved to be.

He stooped and kissed the dead lips, already grown cold.

'Goodbye, Jess,' he said. 'I loved you so much.'

He found a sheet and draped it over her. He left the chalet then and got back into his car. He drove up the track to the hard road and headed back towards Arthurton.

He had to tell Morton that his sister was dead.

The funeral took place with very little delay. She was buried in the graveyard of a little church which the family had attended every Sunday for as long as anyone could remember. There had been a post-mortem, but it had been a formality; the cause of death was all too obvious. The murder weapon had not been found; probably it had been carried away by the man who had used it.

The funeral was well attended, many of the mourners being Morton's police colleagues. Devon thought he detected a kind of accusation in the glances cast at him. He felt that he rather than the unknown murderer was the villain of the piece, and it was not a comfortable feeling. He was glad when the ceremony was over and he could get away.

But the chalet was lonely and unwelcoming without Jessica. And now that she had gone he felt no desire to stay longer on the island. Yet he still had several weeks of his posting to serve, and he could not ask for an early return to London just because the girl he had been living with had been murdered.

And besides, he wanted revenge. Now he was as driven as Adam Holt, with whom he had had no contact since the night of the cocaine dump discovery. He supposed that Holt had

heard or read about the murder and would have put two and
two together, although the information concerning the note left
on the body had been suppressed and was known only to a very
few.

Devon had had an interview with Detective Superintendent
Christy and had demanded a weapon.

'My life has been threatened. I think I should be armed like
your other officers.'

Christy admitted the validity of the argument and gave the
necessary order. Devon was issued with a Colt .38 snub-nosed
revolver and a holster. He had had training in the use of small
arms and was a competent marksman.

'But I hope,' Christy said, 'you're not going to start a private
war. We can do without that.'

He had given instructions that Devon and Morton were not
to take part in the murder investigation. He said they were too
closely involved and he feared it might mar their judgement.
They could not be trusted to act with the cool calculation of
men who had no connection with the unfortunate victim.
Morton dismissed this as a load of bullshit and seemed pretty
angry at being denied the opportunity to run to earth his sister's
killer.

Instead, the investigation was handed over to Detective
Inspector Christian Horler and a small team of subordinates.

'Which is as good as saying the case don't rate much,' Morton
said. 'Like that dead body on the beach. Just forget it.'

'Are you going to forget it?' Devon asked.

'Like hell I am. She was my sister. Somebody's gotta be made to pay.'

Morton and Devon were still partners, but relations between them were a trifle strained, and Devon knew the reason. Finally he decided that things could not be allowed to go on in this way; he had to have it out with Morton.

'You blame me, don't you, Duke?'

'Blame you, Frank?'

'For her death.'

Morton said nothing.

'Look,' Devon said, 'we've got to get things straight. I know very well now that if I hadn't got myself mixed up with that cocaine business she would still be alive today. But I wasn't to know, was I? And if we could only set the clock back and have the time over again I'd certainly not do it all the same way. God knows I wouldn't have wanted to bring any harm to her. You've got to believe me, Duke; I really loved her.'

Morton looked at him in silence for a few moments. Then he said: 'I guess you did at that. I think she musta loved you too.'

'She said she did.'

'You an' me,' Morton said, 'we gotta do somethin' about it. No use leavin' it to that Christian Horler.'

'So we're partners again?'

'We're partners,' Morton said.

Chapter Fourteen

PRESSING INVITATION

But it was the other side that made the first move.

It was evening and Devon was alone in the chalet when the door burst open and two men walked in. They had guns.

Devon was sitting in an armchair and his own Colt was lying on a side-table just out of reach. He made a move to get it, and one of the men said sharply:

'Don't!'

Devon checked his movement and sat back in the chair, because he could see that there was no way he could get the revolver and use it before one or both of the intruders pumped some little bits of metal into him that would do his body no good at all.

He recognized the man who had spoken. It was the gate-keeper with the moustache whom he and Morton had encountered on the occasion of their visit to the house of Mr Jorge Ramirez. The other man was smaller, swarthy, black hair retreating from the forehead and pony-tailed at the back. The most prominent feature about him was his nose, which was almost of the proportions of Cyrano de Bergerac's. Devon was no more favourably impressed by this man than by the one with the moustache. In his mind they were both classified as villains.

'What do you want?' he asked.

'You,' the moustache said.

'And suppose I'm not available?'

'Don't play games,' the moustache said. 'You come with us to see Mr Ramirez. He want to speak to you.'

The nose said nothing; he just stood there looking evil and handling a big automatic pistol as if he just longed to be using it on someone; preferably Devon.

'Now why should Mr Ramirez wish to have a talk with me?' Devon said. 'We're not old pals. I hardly know the man.'

'He know you. So you coming?'

'Suppose I were to decline the invitation. What then? Do you shoot me? That would hardly please Mr Ramirez if he wishes to see me.'

'You don't come quiet, we take you,' the moustache said. 'You want it that way?'

Devon was quite sure he did not want it that way. He was not foolish enough to believe that any good would come from resisting these men. They had come to get him and, one way or another, they would do so. It was the same old choice between the hard way and the easy way. He chose the latter.

'Very well,' he said. 'Let's go and hear what the man has to say for himself.'

*

They had left their car just off the hard road; perhaps in order not to give him any warning of their approach. It was a big white Mercedes-Benz.

The moustache drove. Devon and the nose sat in the back. The nose kept his pistol in his hand, though it was quite unnecessary; Devon had no intention of trying to jump out of a moving car. That was as good a way as any of getting yourself a broken leg, or even a bullet in the back.

Ramirez was waiting for him in the room where he and Morton had been taken to question the woman named Inez. There was no sign of her on this occasion. Nor was Dolores, the wife, anywhere to be seen. Obviously it was to be a man to man talk.

'Ah, Mr Devon,' Ramirez said. 'I am so glad you were able to come.'

'How could I refuse?' Devon said. 'The invitation was so pressing.'

The moustache and the nose had come in with him, but now Ramirez dismissed them with a wave of the hand. They left the room and closed the door behind them, but Devon had no doubt that they would remain close at hand.

'I hope,' Ramirez said, 'you were not in any way manhandled. I'm afraid my men can sometimes be rather over-zealous.'

'They didn't have to be. I took the hint.'

'I see that you are a sensible man. Will you have a drink?'

'No thank you,' Devon said. 'Let's not pretend that this is a social visit. You and I both know damn well it isn't anything of the sort. You want something from me. What is it?'

Ramirez came swiftly to the point. 'The name and whereabouts of your associate.'

'His name is Morton. But you knew that already. He was here with me before.'

Ramirez made a little gesture of impatience. 'You know that was not what I was asking. I was referring to the man who was with you the other night when the two of you made some trouble at Salt Cove.'

'Ah!' Devon said. And he was thinking that here was the confirmation of what he had only suspected until then: that Ramirez was at the heart of the cocaine smuggling organisation. He was no doubt the St Joseph representative of one of the Colombian gangs which were so wealthy and powerful that they had their private armies and could even challenge the legitimate government. He was thinking also that Ramirez had to be very sure of himself if he was prepared to reveal so much to a member, if only a temporary one, of the Arthurton police force. Now that was really something to reflect upon, and one had to ask oneself how deeply the influence of this man had penetrated the fabric of St Joseph society. How much of it had become corrupted?

'I notice,' Ramirez said, 'that you do not deny the fact that you were there.'

'And I notice,' Devon replied, 'that you do not conceal the fact that you know all about it.'

Ramirez gave a laugh. 'Well, that clears the air, doesn't it? Now we both know just where we stand.'

He was in fact not standing, but was seated in a leather upholstered armchair. He appeared totally at ease; he was smoking a cigar and the aroma of it pervaded the room.

'I had suspicions about you from the start,' Devon said. 'I can usually recognise a crook when I see one.'

Ramirez frowned. He said: 'A man in your position should be careful what he says. It is hardly in your interest to insult me.'

'You think it's an insult? You surprise me. I should have thought that to a man like you it would have seemed a compliment. After all, you've made a great success of your chosen profession, to judge by these surroundings.'

'You can omit the sarcasm; it's of no benefit to you. Let's get back to the serious business. Who was the man with you at Salt Cove and where do I find him?'

'As to his name,' Devon said, 'that's of no importance. I could give you one and you wouldn't know whether it was the right one or false. So I'll not bother. And as to finding him, well, the short answer is that you don't.'

'You are refusing to tell me where he is?'

'I don't have the choice. I don't know myself.'

'And you expect me to believe that?'

'Believe it or not; it happens to be the truth. He refused to tell me.'

'Why?'

'He seemed to have the odd idea that if I didn't know I

couldn't tell anyone else. Like you for instance. He was just being cautious. With reason. A colleague of his was shot in the head and his body dumped on a beach. But perhaps you know all about that.'

Ramirez did not say whether he did or not. He said: 'If you don't know where he is, how do you get in touch with him?'

'I don't. He gets in touch with me. When he feels it's necessary to do so.'

'I still find this very hard to believe,' Ramirez said. He drew some smoke from the cigar and let it drift away from his mouth. He looked at Devon reflectively. 'I am debating in my mind whether or not it might be a good plan to try some persuasion on you.'

Devon glanced towards the door. 'You're thinking of calling in the heavies and letting them get to work on me? It wouldn't be any use. Not because I'm a particularly tough nut to crack, but because I simply don't know the answer to your question.'

Ramirez said: 'You're treading a very dangerous path, you know. I don't think you're taking much notice of the warning you found in your chalet. That girl was very beautiful, I'm told. A pity she—'

He got no further, because Devon rushed at him and struck him a blow with his right hand on the angle of the jaw which knocked him sideways in the chair and would certainly have sent him to the floor if the arm had not saved him. Before he could recover Devon had hit him on the other side of the jaw, which straightened him up and put him in position to take a clenched fist in the pit of the stomach. Devon would have gone on hitting him until he had reduced him to a bloody wreck, such was his fury at that sneering mention of the killing of Jessica which had surely touched him on the raw and was tantamount to a confession that the man had ordered it even if he had not carried it out himself. But he was not allowed to go to this extreme, because Ramirez was yelling like mad, and in a moment the moustache and the nose were in the room.

He felt himself seized from behind, one man to an arm, and then they were hauling him away from the chair and handling him very roughly indeed. He struggled to break away from them, but they were too much for him. He might have dealt with one at a time, but not the two of them together.

Ramirez had dropped his cigar in the attack, and now he was getting up from the chair with a murderous look in his eye. From somewhere or other he produced a small nickel-plated automatic. He walked across to the pinioned Devon and jabbed him in the forehead with the muzzle of the pistol, the index finger of his right hand curled around the trigger.

'You're a dead man,' he said in a cold hard voice.

Devon believed him. He was shaking with rage and the pistol was grinding into Devon's head. Just a little more pressure from that index finger and a bullet would shatter his skull and that would be the end of things for him. One thing was certain: Ramirez could not miss the target; ranges never came any closer than this. There was always a chance that the gun might misfire or jam, but it would be foolish to put much hope in that.

And then the telephone started ringing.

Ramirez hestitated. He seemed to be debating in his mind whether to do the killing first and then answer the call or to postpone driving a bullet into Devon's brain until he had discovered who it was that was calling. In the end he chose the latter course, and Devon breathed again. It was a case of being saved by the bell. But for how long? It could well be no more than a reprieve.

The telephone was on a desk by the wall. Ramirez walked over to it, laid the pistol down and lifted the receiver.

'Yes?'

A pause while he listened to someone speaking at the other end of the line. Then:

'Yes, he's here now.'

Another pause. Then:

'No, he has not. He doesn't know. Or says he doesn't. And he has attacked me. For which he will be made to pay.'

A pause again. Then angrily:

'Why not? He is of no importance.'

A longer pause. Then finally, and with more anger:

'Very well, Ve–ry well.'

He slammed the receiver down, picked up the pistol and walked back to where Devon was still being held by the two heavies. He pressed the muzzle of the pistol again on Devon's forehead, and again his finger was on the trigger. But he did not fire the gun. Suddenly he lowered it and spat in Devon's face. He followed this with a slap on each cheek, first with the palm of his hand and then with the back. Finally he clenched his right fist and drove it hard into Devon's stomach.

It hurt. It hurt damnably. All the wind seemed to have been driven out of his body and he was left gasping and retching.

Ramirez still had the pistol in his left hand, and he seemed half inclined to use it after all. There was venom in his expression and it was obvious that he was having difficulty in controlling his passion. But with an effort he succeeded. He turned away, went back to his chair and sat down.

The men holding Devon had not spoken and had not moved. They were waiting for orders. And the orders came in a snarl.

'Take him away. Take him out of my sight.'

It was the moustache who asked the question: 'Where do we take him?'

'Back to where you found him. Back to his kennel. What are you waiting for?'

They moved quickly then. They bundled Devon out of the room, out of the house and into the car. Again the moustache drove and the nose sat in the back with the passenger. They were saying nothing. They seemed much surprised at the turn of events, but they had had their orders and were carrying them out.

Devon was surprised too – and greatly relieved. He was also puzzled; for there could be no doubt that it was the telephone call that had saved his life. But for that, Ramirez would certainly have shot him. So who could have been on the other end of the line? It had to be someone who had had prior knowledge of that meeting in Ramirez's house and had an interest in the outcome of the interrogation. Someone who had immediately guessed what Ramirez had meant by the words: 'For which he will pay.' Someone who had then forbidden it. Who could have possessed that knowledge and that authority? Not many people could have controlled the furious Colombian with a word.

He thought about it as the Mercedes rolled smoothly on its way; and suddenly, quite without warning, a name floated into his consciousness: Edgar Roylance, Minister for the Interior and Justice.

It came as a shock. He could not believe it. He thrust it away, but it came back; it would not leave him. In his mind he had a picture of that lean, pockmarked, greying man in the dark glasses, the immaculate suit and the snakeskin shoes. A man with undoubted authority. A man who could order people around. Even Jorge Ramirez? Perhaps even him. A man to whom the death of a young and innocent woman would be of little consequence, but for whom the murder on the island of a visiting British police officer might have been an acute embarrassment; one that he had no wish to experience.

So if the unthinkable was in fact very much the thinkable and Edgar Roylance had a finger in the cocaine racket, who else was involved? Or, more to the point, who was not involved? The more he thought about it, the more he felt like a man struggling in a morass; and the more he struggled, the less hope there seemed to be of freeing himself.

So why bother? He had not been sent to St Joseph to clean up widespread corruption. According to Detective Superintendent Lee it was to have been a holiday in the sun. So why not let it be just that? Why not stick to his brief and do what the note on the dead body had advised? Why not keep his nose out?

Well, for one thing, simply because of that dead body. He had loved the girl and he had a burning desire to make the killers pay. And that included Jorge Ramirez, who might not have done the throat slitting himself but had certainly given the order for it to be done. And one of these two gorillas in the car had no doubt done the job. As to which one had actually carried out the killing was immaterial; in his book they were both guilty.

They came to the dirt road leading to the chalet. The moustache stopped the car. Devon got out and said:

'I won't thank you for the ride. It wasn't a pleasure and I hope it won't ever be repeated. But I expect to see you again, because there's an account to settle. And settled it will be, sooner or later.'

The moustache said: 'You're lucky to be alive. Don't push it, señor. You better remember the warning.'

'Oh, I'll remember it,' Devon said. 'You can be sure of that.'

He slammed the car door and walked away. Behind him he could hear the Merc being turned and driven off.

Chapter Fifteen

MOLOTOV COCKTAILS

He wondered who he should tell. He wondered whether he should tell anyone. He could have gone to Detective Inspector Horler and informed him that he knew who was responsible for the murder which Horler and his team were supposed to be investigating. But would it have been of any use? He thought not. He wondered whether there was anyone he could trust.

In the end he decided to tell Morton. Because Morton had as much interest in the matter as he had. It was his sister who had been murdered.

He left it until the morning when they were in Morton's car, going about their normal business, which for the present had little interest for either of them. Morton listened to the story in silence until Devon stopped speaking. Then he said:

'So now we know the whole of it.'

'Yes. We know the bastards who killed Jess and we know who gave the order.'

'That man—' Morton said; and then seemed lost for words to

express his feelings adequately. A stream of invective might have been expected, but nothing came. A tightening of the jaw was the only visible sign of any emotion. But Devon was conscious of the immeasurable anger that was possessing him.

'You didn't know Ramirez was involved in the drug smuggling racket?'

'No.'

'But you must have known it was going on.'

'Well, yes. We all knew something of the sort was on the go, but it was something we were not encouraged to look at too closely. Jus' keep our eyes shut to it and get on with our jobs. It was all too big for us, see? Too many powerful folks with a finger in the pie.'

'Including Edgar Roylance?'

'Mebbe. I don't know. Why him in particular?'

'I think he may be a big player. One of the biggest.'

'You do? Well, could be.'

'Question is, what do we do about Ramirez and the other two?'

Morton answered calmly, as though it were a question that scarcely needed thinking about: 'We kill them.'

'It could be difficult.'

'To hell with difficulty. They killed my sister. They killed Jessie. They slit her throat. Don't that mean nothin' to you?'

'It means everything,' Devon said.

'So are you with me or ain't you?'

'I'm with you, Duke. All the way.'

*

Adam Holt turned up again that evening. It was about ten o'clock. He came to the chalet. He had heard about Jessica's death and he said how sorry he was.

'It's another score to settle.'

'But not for you, Adam. This one's a family matter.'

'Sure, sure. But they kinda converge.'

He turned quickly to the business that had brought him there.

'The Catalina's back again.'

It transpired that he had been keeping a watch on Salt Cove and had seen the flying boat arrive that afternoon. He had watched another batch of cocaine being unloaded and carried away by the mules.

'It's still there. It'll be there all night. This is our chance.'

'Chance for what?'

'To make our hit. Are you game?'

'I'm game,' Devon said. After what had happened recently he would have been game for anything that was calculated to strike at Ramirez and the others. 'What's the plan?'

Holt told him. It sounded good.

'When do we start?'

'Soon as you're ready. You got yourself a gun yet?'

'I've got a gun,' Devon said.

They went in Holt's car. They drove through Arthurton and out on to the coast road. They followed the road to Logan's Bay, but did not stop there. About a mile beyond Logan's Bay they came to a place where a stony track led down to a small beach. At that time of night it was deserted. The moon was now past the full, but there was enough of it left to give some light; enough for their purpose.

Holt stopped the car near the top of the track, and from the boot he hauled out a large package and an outboard motor, which they carried down to the beach. The package was an inflatable dinghy with a couple of paddles. They set these burdens down and went back to the car. There was a wooden box with rope handles in the back, and this they also carried down to the beach, together with a small axe. When they had inflated the dinghy and put the box in and fixed the outboard to the stern they carried it down to where the sea was lapping the shore and showing a line of white foam. They launched it on to the small waves and pushed it out until the water was almost up to their waists. They got in then and paddled it into deeper water. The sea was calm and they had no difficulty.

Holt started the motor and they were away, heading southwards along the coast.

'A fine night for it,' Devon said. He could feel a slight fluttering sensation in the stomach and he wondered whether Holt was feeling the same. The American seemed utterly calm, but you never could tell. Perhaps to Holt he himself appeared nerveless. 'I just hope the Cat's still there.'

'You can count on that,' Holt said.

The coastline slid past on the port side and there was no sound but the chatter of the outboard motor and the swish-

swish-swish of water sweeping by. The air had a pleasant fresh-
ness in it, and Devon could not help reflecting that, had it not
been for the knowledge of the kind of errand they were on, it
would have been an enjoyable trip. It was the thought of what
was to come that took the pleasure out of it. Things could go
wrong; they could go disastrously wrong. Though neither of
them had mentioned the fact, they knew that they were putting
their lives on the line.

'This is it,' Holt said.

They had come to Salt Cove. Devon could see the gap in the
shoreline that was the mouth of the inlet. Holt cut the motor
and the dinghy ceased to surge forward.

'From here it's paddle time,' he said. 'We don't want to
announce our arrival. Let it be a surprise to them.'

They took up their paddles and began to propel the dinghy
into the cove. Soon the shape of the flying boat appeared as a
dark mass in the gloom, with just a single mooring light visible.
If there were people inside it, they seemed to have gone to bed.

'All quiet on the Western Front,' Holt murmured.

A little later they had reached the Catalina. The dinghy
touched the hull with scarcely a sound and Holt made it fast to
one of the wing struts with the painter.

Devon climbed on to the hull just forward of the wing and
Holt passed the axe up to him. From his perch he was within
easy reach of the transparent roof of the cockpit. This was
constructed of panes of perspex and he immediately began hack-
ing at it with the axe. It was tough material and not as easy a task

as he had imagined it might be. But he wielded the axe with vigour and suddenly one of the panes broke away from the metal framework, leaving a gaping hole in the cover.

Meanwhile, Holt had opened the box to reveal that inside it were half a dozen petrol bombs of the kind once known as Molotov cocktails. They were simply glass bottles filled with petrol and with a cloth wick plugging the neck.

He called up to Devon: 'Ready yet, Frank?'

'Ready.'

But the activity with the axe had not gone unnoticed inside the Catalina. Lights were now showing and a man came into the cockpit. Devon could see him from his perch and observed that the man had a gun in his hand. He spotted the broken cover immediately, and looked up and saw Devon. He was not a man to bother with asking questions in a situation of this sort; he simply raised the pistol and fired through the hole.

Devon jerked his head back just in time, and the bullet whistled past far too close for comfort. He waited for no second shot but slid down the hull and into the dinghy, which rocked alarmingly as his weight came on it and shipped some water. Holt had not been inactive during this piece of business. He had taken a cigarette-lighter from his pocket and had ignited the wick of one of the petrol bombs. Now he reached up and lobbed it into the cockpit through the hole that Devon had made.

The result was impressive: a burst of flame and a scream from the man with the gun. Holt followed up quickly with a second petrol bomb and yelled at Devon to release the painter. While

Devon was doing this he started the motor, and a few moments later the dinghy was scudding away from the flying boat and heading for the jetty.

Looking back, Devon could see that the petrol bombs had really taken effect. Flames were shooting up from the cockpit and casting a garish light on the water of the cove. He could see nothing of the man with the gun or any other occupants of the flying boat. If they managed to get away from the blazing aircraft they would have to swim for it, unless they had some kind of life-raft. It was not something he was much bothered about; he had little sympathy for men who made their money from the illicit drug trade. And for him and Holt there was more work to be done before their night's task was finished.

Holt was steering the dinghy, but he took a glance back over his shoulder at the floating bonfire behind him.

'Nice job,' he said. 'That's one big bird that won't be returning to its nest tomorrow. And maybe never.'

'Pity it had to be done,' Devon said. 'Can't be many like that left in the world today. Catalinas did a fine job in the war, escorting convoys and that sort of thing.'

'Now don't be getting all sentimental,' Holt said. 'This one had come down in the world. It was doing a dirty job. We're just putting it out of its misery.'

'Maybe you're right.'

'I know I'm right,' Holt said.

They had just reached the jetty when the plane blew up. It made one hell of a racket, and a column of flame and smoke shot up into the air. Bits and pieces descended on the water in a shower of debris, pitting the surface.

'Well now,' Holt said, 'I guess there must have been some gasoline on board to make that old girl go up like that. It sure is curtains for her now.'

'Some show! Like Guy Fawkes' Night back home.'

'I wouldn't know about that,' Holt said. 'But this is no time for us to stand and stare. We better be on our way. Pronto.'

Chapter Sixteen

QUITE A NIGHT

There was no one at the jetty and the beach appeared deserted. They took the box and the axe and set off up the gully. When they came to the top of the cliff they followed the mule track, and soon they were hemmed in by the trees and the undergrowth.

They had not gone far when they heard men coming towards them. The men were running, and as they ran they were gabbling excitedly. Holt and Devon heard them soon enough to get off the track and take cover before they went past. There were three of them, and there could be no doubt that they had heard the explosion and had seen the red glare in the sky. Now they were on their way to see what had happened.

Holt and Devon let them go by, and then returned to the track and went on. When they came to the bowl where the storehouse was they could see no sign of the mules. It seemed probable that beyond the store there was a continuation of the track leading maybe to some houses where the mule drivers lived, and possibly the boatmen too. No doubt that was where the mules were kept. On their previous visit they had made no exploration further than the long wooden shed which had been the object of their search, and in the end they had had to get away fast.

Now when they came to the shed Devon immediately set about smashing windows with the axe, two on each side. Holt followed up with the remaining petrol bombs, tossing one in at each of these four places. The boarding of the shed must have been like tinder, dry and highly inflammable. Very soon the entire store was ablaze and the timber was crackling as it burned.

It was a splendid fire, and the two men who had started it were inclined to linger and admire their handiwork, though the intense heat drove them to a respectable distance from the flames. So intent were they on watching this most gratifying sight that neither of them was immediately aware that they were no longer the only observers of the fire. Quite a a little crowd had appeared in the clearing: women, children and a few men as well. It was evident from this that there must have been a number of dwellings not far away, and this was merely confirmation of what they had already guessed. No doubt all these people, if they had been asleep, had been awakened by the explosion of the Catalina and had then been drawn by this raging bonfire so much nearer at hand.

There was much excitement among them, and the shouting of the children could be heard above the crackling of the flames. It occurred to Devon that for some if not all of these people the twin fires of aircraft and storehouse might well be a disaster. Many of them might be dependent on the drug trade for their livelihood, for it was obviously not only those at the top who benefited from the racket, even though it was they who skimmed off the cream. Others who did the menial work of fetching and carrying got their share also.

'I think we'd better go,' he said. 'I'd say we're not going to be terribly popular with that lot if they catch sight of us. They'll guess we started the bonfire.'

'I think you're dead right,' Holt said. 'Let's be on our way.'

But already they had been spotted, and a yell went up from the little knot of people. Almost immediately three men detached themselves from the group and started running towards them. Two of these were carrying machetes, and all three might have been remembering that not many days previously one of the mule drivers had been shot by intruders. It would not have taken any great amount of thinking to connect the fire-raisers with that earlier incident, and here were the two men obviously responsible for setting the storehouse alight.

Without more ado Holt and Devon turned and ran, heading for the track by which they had come. The men came pounding after them, yelling blood-curdling threats as they came. The two fugitives were still climbing the slope from the hollow and had not yet reached the cover of the trees when they heard the crack of a pistol, which was very good evidence that the third pursuer, the one without a machete, had a potentially even more lethal weapon, and was using it.

Devon glanced back and saw that this man had stopped running and was taking aim again, but he must have come to the conclusion that if he fired he was as likely to hit one of his companions as the chosen target, for he did not shoot again.

The men with the machetes were good runners and they were very close now. Either Devon or Holt might have turned and taken a shot at them, but this could not have been done in an instant, and the risk of being slashed by a machete was too great to accept.

They came to the top of the slope and continued running along the mule track, Holt just ahead of Devon and the two men with the machetes close behind. The one with the pistol had taken up the pursuit again too, but he was several yards behind and practically out of sight in the gloom.

Devon was breathing hard and had a pain in the side. He doubted whether he could keep up the pace much longer, and the pursuers were certainly not being left behind. He had a nasty feeling that at any moment one of those machetes might slice into him just between the shoulder-blades, which would not be at all good for his health.

So he struggled on and wondered when Holt would make a move to get off the mule track, since it would not be at all helpful to their cause if they got themselves too close to the cove and met the men who had gone that way coming back to see what it was that was lighting up the sky where they had come from.

And then just that happened. They rounded a bend in the track and ran slap-bang into those very men. For a moment all was confusion. The men from the cove were taken by surprise and made no attempt to seize the fugitives, while the pursuers, coming up fast from behind, could not use the machetes because in the mêlée and the gloom they might as easily have carved up a black man as a white.

In this crisis Holt was the quickest thinker. With a shout to Devon to follow him, he got himself free from the mix-up and plunged into the jungle on the right of the track. Devon lost no time in following him, narrowly avoiding the swing of a machete which came within inches of slicing off his left arm. He heard the swish of it as it went past, and it must have hit a tree and jarred the wielder's hand, for he gave a cry of pain and anger.

Devon could hear Holt scrambling through the undergrowth just ahead of him and he followed the sound. In the confusion they had opened up a gap between themselves and the pursuit, but they were running blindly and were in constant danger of being tripped by some unseen obstruction like a trailing creeper or the root of a tree. Devon knew that a fall could prove fatal, because the hunt would be on to them in a moment.

This thought had no sooner come into his head than the very thing he feared happened. Holt stumbled and fell. Devon, brought to an abrupt stop, acted by instinct rather than cool calculation. He turned to face the oncoming pursuit, and the snub-nosed revolver was in his hand in an instant. He started firing at once, not pausing to take aim. He loosed off four or five shots in quick succession and heard a man give a scream and knew that he had halted them all for the moment.

Holt's voice came to him with a note of urgency: 'Okay, Frankie; let's go, let's go.'

The American was on his feet again and running. Devon turned and ran after him.

The pursuit appeared to be in some confusion now that one of the number had been wounded; how badly it was impossible to say. The others seemed to have lost some eagerness to be at the head of the chase and hesitated to start running again. The one with the gun fired a few times, but he was doing it blindly and the bullets ripped harmlessly into the foliage and timber.

Devon just hoped Holt had some sense of direction. One thing was certain: they would not be returning by the way they had come. The dinghy had served its purpose and must be left to whoever cared to claim it. Somehow, Devon did not think that person would be Adam Holt.

Holt stopped and allowed Devon to come up with him. There was now no sound of any pursuit; the Colt revolver had taken some of the enthusiasm out of the hunters. Devon could hear voices, but they were faint and evidently some distance away.

'Guess you took some of the sass out of them with that gun of yours. What is it?'

'Colt thirty-eight.'

'Ah! Handy little weapon. You sure saved my bacon back there. I could have been sliced meat. I'm beholden to you.'

'I was saving my own bacon too.'

'So we both better be grateful to you. And glad you brought the shooter along with you.'

'Well, we'd best not stand here gabbing away. You know which way to head?'

There was very little light getting through the foliage, and it would have been easy to wander around in circles and possibly bump into the hunters – if any were still hunting.

'We need to get to the road,' Holt said.

'True. But which way is it?'

'East, I reckon.'

'So all we need is a compass. You got one?'

'No. But if we move away from those voices it should be the right direction. Come on.'

He set off again and Devon followed. Ten minutes later, more by luck than judgement, they found the road.

'I was right,' Holt said, taking all the credit.

'So you were right. Now all we have to do is go back to the car.'

This was the easy part. There was not much traffic on the road. When a vehicle came along they took cover pretty smartly, because they had no wish to be seen and were certainly not going to try thumbing a lift. In the distance they could see that one fire at least was still burning; it was a red glare in the sky. The roof of the storehouse had probably collapsed on the merchandise stowed beneath.

'Will cocaine burn?' Devon asked.

'I don't know,' Holt said. 'But the bags will, and my guess is that what's left will never be fit to go on the market; it'll be too messed up. Nobody would buy it.'

'So we've done a good night's work.'

'You could say that.'

The car was where they had left it. It was in the small hours when Holt left Devon at the chalet.

'I doubt whether we shall be meeting again,' he said. 'The work is done. Of course you know and I know it's no more than a dent in the narcotics trade. But it's something. I'm grateful for your help. I'd have had difficulty managing on my own.'

'Glad to lend a hand,' Devon said. But he was thinking that it had been at some cost. The empty chalet would remind him of that as soon as he stepped inside. 'My job isn't finished yet, though. There's still a score to settled.'

'Ah!' Holt said.

Devon thought of asking him to give some help with that. A quid pro quo. But he decided not to. It was something for him and Morton to do, with no assistance from anyone else. It was a personal thing.

'Well, so long,' Holt said. 'Take care.'

He turned the car and drove away.

Devon went into the chalet and made a cup of coffee. He sat for a long time, drinking coffee and thinking. He felt no inclination to sleep. One way and another it had been quite a night.

Chapter Seventeen

SMALL PROBLEM

He was somewhat bleary-eyed when he joined Morton in the morning. He had finally dropped off to sleep sitting in an armchair, and he had waked after a few hours, stiff and dry-mouthed. He had taken a shower and put on fresh clothes and drunk more coffee and eaten breakfast cereal. And now he was feeling, if not quite a new person, at least something of an improvement on the one that had started the day.

'There's a rumour going round,' Morton said, 'that some sort of incident occurred at Salt Cove last night. You wouldn't know anything about that, would you?'

Devon was surprised that it had not got into the papers, or at least on the radio. He guessed that certain powerful people had no wish for it to be publicised, and had put a clamp on the news. Censorship was obviously alive and kicking in this little corner of the world. But word got around regardless.

'I might,' Devon said.

'Would I be a mile off the mark if I suggested you were involved in what took place?'

'Not even half a mile.'

'You really do stick your neck out, don't you, Frank? Who was with you?'

'You don't think it was a single-handed job?'

'Way I heard it, there was a flying boat blown up and a big storehouse full of cocaine torched. That sound to you like a one-man job?'

'I'd say not.'

'So who was helping you?'

Devon came to the conclusion that he could trust Morton in this. And besides, the presence of Holt on the island was known to those in authority. The wonder was that he had managed for so long to preserve his freedom – and his life. It just showed what a clever operator he was; one really smart guy.

'An American acquaintance. And it was I who was helping him, not the other way round. It was his baby.'

'A Yank without a name, huh?'

'What's in a name?' Devon said.

'You plannin' to do any more mayhem alonga him?'

'No. It's finished. It's my guess that if he hasn't left the island already he damn soon will have. I don't expect to see him again. Ever.'

'Maybe it's as well for you, you don't,' Morton said. 'But we've still got that other business to clear up. And I don't think we should wait any longer. I think we should do it tonight.'

'You got a plan?'

'Yes. I been thinkin' about it, and seems to me there's only one way to handle it. The simple way. No frills and no complications.'

'Tell me,' Devon said.

Morton told him. 'We drive up to the gate. When the gatekeeper comes out we shoot him. Then we ram the gate with the car. If that don't do the trick we climb over. We go up to the house and shoot Ramirez.'

It was undoubtedly a simple plan, and there were certainly no frills. Whether or not there would be any complications was quite another matter.

'What you think, Frank?'

'Could work. Couple of questions. What if Ramirez is not at home? And what about the other gorilla?'

'No problem. We ring up first with some cock and bull story to make sure he's there. The other bastard? We kill him anyway.'

'Clean sweep, eh?'

'You said it. Clean sweep. They got it comin'.'

Devon thought of the women. It would be pretty nasty for them, but that was just too bad. One thing could be counted on: they would not interfere.

'You still ready to go through with it?' Morton asked. 'No second thoughts? No cold feet?'

'None. My feet are as warm as ever.'

'So it's settled. I'll come for you this evening. We'll go in my car. Don't forget your gun.'

'As if I would!'

Morton turned up at around eight o'clock in his Rover. Devon wondered whether it would be powerful enough to burst open the gates to Ramirez's stronghold. They had appeared to be pretty solid. Maybe a Land-Rover would have been more suitable for the job. Or a bulldozer. He had a feeling that they would have to do the climb.

'You checked whether Ramirez was in?'

'I checked. He's there.'

Morton seemed calm. For a man who was setting out to commit murder he was showing remarkably little emotion. But no doubt he regarded it as an execution rather than murder. As Devon himself did. It was to be a piece of just retribution.

'Good night for it,' Morton said. 'No rain. Best that way.'

There had in fact been a brief tropical shower earlier in the day; it had come and gone in a few minutes, and then the sun had dried up all evidence of it as if with a magic wand.

Devon was feeling edgy and hoping it was not noticeable. To kill someone in cold blood was way out of his experience. Maybe it was out of Morton's too. Yet again he told himself it would not be murder but justice. He conjured up the picture in his mind of Jessica with her slashed throat, and it hardened his resolve; steeled him for what he had to do. No man should be allowed to get away with that. And it was of no use leaving matters to the Arthurton police.

Morton drove in silence. Neither of them felt inclined to make small-talk. The journey did not take long. Soon they were in that select part of Arthurton on the slopes overlooking the town; a quiet district where only the rich could afford to live.

Morton slowed the car as they approached the entrance to Ramirez's place. And then the headlights picked out the pillars on each side of the gateway. But when they reached the entrance they found no gatekeeper and the gates were wide open.

'This is odd,' Morton said. He had stopped the car and the lights revealed a deserted drive. 'What in hell's happened?'

'Somebody forgot to lock up?'

'No chance.'

'Well, one thing's certain. We don't have to ram the gates and we don't have to climb over them. Makes it easier for us. I suggest we leave the car just inside and walk the rest of the way. Don't want to give Ramirez any warning he's got visitors.'

Morton agreed with this. He drove the car inside, stopped it and switched off the engine and lights. Both men got out, Morton carrying a torch to light the way. They turned the bend in the drive and the shadowy mass of the house loomed up ahead.

'Now here's another odd thing,' Devon said. 'No lights.'

Indeed, there was not a light showing, either in the house or outside. It was all dark and rather eerie. They came to a halt and stared at the building. On one side, Devon remembered, there was the swimming-pool, where they had found Dolores Ramirez sunning herself on the first occasion he had been there. It was dark there too. On his second visit he recalled it had all been lit up, without and within. Ramirez seemed to abhor darkness. So why was it dark now?

'Can't have gone to bed this early,' Morton said. 'Something's wrong. I can feel it.'

Devon felt it too. Only the most insensitive of men could have failed to do so.

'Well,' he said, 'it's no use just standing here. Better go and take a look inside.'

They climbed the steps to the portico and came to the doorway by which they had entered before. And here yet another oddity was revealed by the beam of Morton's torch. The door was slightly ajar, as though someone might have left the house in haste and omitted to close it behind him.

They went inside. Morton was holding the torch in his left hand and his pistol in the other. Devon had the revolver in his right hand. Morton let the beam of the torch explore the spacious entrance hall. Nothing suspicious was revealed and there was dead silence in the house. Not a thing seemed to be stirring.

'Let's try some more of the rooms,' Morton said. He was keeping his voice low, as if afraid of being overheard, though there was no evidence of anyone listening. 'Must be somebody here.'

'Unless it's another *Mary Celeste*,' Devon said.

'What you talkin' about?'

'A sailing ship found drifting at sea abandoned by the crew.'

'We don't know the house has been abandoned.'

'Maybe it's a trap.'

'How could it be? Nobody knew we were coming.'

'That's true.'

'Oh hell! Let's not stand here jabbering. Let's go see what we can find.'

There was a door to one of the other ground floor rooms standing open. They followed the narrow beam of Morton's torch into it. Morton tripped over something lying on the floor and cursed. He lowered the beam and saw what had tripped him and swore again.

'Jesus Christ!'

It was the young black maid. She had been shot and was dead. They could see the bullet holes and the blood.

Devon found the switch and flooded the room with light. Only then did they become aware of the extent of the slaughter. Ramirez was lying on his back, and there was blood all over the front of his shirt where he had been stabbbed many times. It looked as though he had been attacked by someone in a mad frenzy, and there was no doubt about the weapon that had been used because it was still sticking in the body. It was a cook's knife with a long blade. Probably tapering to a point, which was at present hidden in Ramirez's flesh.

There were two other bodies lying on the floor. One was that of Dolores Ramirez and the other was Inez, whom Ramirez had introduced to them as his housekeeper; the one who had made the garbled call to police headquarters with the information that someone or other was being killed. Both these women appeared to have been shot.

Morton sucked his teeth. 'Now here's a mess.' He looked at the bloody corpse of Ramirez. 'Somebody beat us to it. Now who could that have been?'

Devon pointed at the woman with the half Indian look about her and the hooked nose, 'My guess is it was her.'

'But why?'

'Well, this is guessing again, but here's a possible sequence of events. Ramirez is knocking his wife about again. Inez hears her screams and decides to put an end to that sort of thing once and for all. Maybe she's been with Dolores for a long time and has a motherly feeling for her. Maybe she just hates Ramirez's guts anyway. So she snatches up the knife and runs in here and lets him have it good and proper. How does that strike you for a possibility?'

'Could be. But who shot the women?'

'That's easy. It has to be the two gorillas. They could have been near at hand, heard Ramirez yelling and came in at the double, but too late to save him.'

'And shot the housekeeper in revenge?'

'Seems possible. Though I doubt they had that much feeling for the boss.'

'Why shoot the wife too?'

'Well, look at it this way, from their point of view. They come in here, and there's their meal ticket lying dead on the floor. Straightaway they start working out in their mean little minds just how this will affect them. And it doesn't take them long to decide that it's in their best interest to snatch what they can lay their grubby hands on and scarper. Have another look at Dolores. See anything odd about her, apart from the bullet holes and the blood?'

Morton looked at the corpse for few moments and then said: 'No jewellery.'

Devon nodded. 'No rings, no bangles, no necklace, no earrings. And last time I was here Ramirez was wearing a gold wristwatch that must have been worth thousands. It's gone.'

'They could have taken the loot without killing the women.'

'They're Colombians,' Devon said. 'Killing just comes natural to them. And they wouldn't have wanted anyone giving the alarm while they were filling their pockets.'

'And the maid?'

'Probably just walked in to see what was going on. So they shot her too. She was simply out of luck.'

'We better take a look round,' Morton said.

'Let's do that.'

In the room where Ramirez had interviewed Devon they found that the desk had been ransacked, drawers pulled out, papers scattered around, everything in disorder.

'Wonder if they found anything valuable in there,' Morton said. 'You ask me, there'll be a safe somewhere, but they wouldn't know the combination 'cause Ramirez likely kept it in his head. Any large amount of cash will be in there; you can bet your life on that. He couldn't take it with him, but he sure could take the secret.'

They went up a wide carpeted stairway to the next floor. In one of the bedrooms they found a dressing-table loaded with toiletry of the most expensive kind. The room had an odour which would have told them even blindfold who had occupied it. The furnishing was opulent and a door opened on to a bathroom of equal luxury.

There was a gilded box on the dressing-table. It was open and it was velvet-lined. A tray, also lined with velvet, had been taken out and was lying beside it where some of the bottles and jars had been pushed aside to make room for it. Both tray and box were empty.

'This musta been her jewel-box,' Morton said. 'Wonder how much the stuff was worth.'

'Plenty, I'd say. Man like Ramirez wouldn't have his wife wearing trash.'

They went back downstairs.

Morton said: 'We have a small problem here.'

'What's that?'

'What do we do now?'

'You don't think we could just leave and say nothing? Let somebody else find this mess?'

'It's an attractive suggestion. Yes, very attractive. But it's not really on. Bloody hell, Frank, when all's said and done we're still police officers. We can't walk away from this.'

Reluctantly, Devon had to agree.

'You going to use the phone here?'

'Might as well,' Morton said.

Chapter Eighteen

HELP FROM SPIDER

Morton put the call through to Christy's home because at that time in the evening the detective superintendent would be off duty. It was Mrs Christy who answered the phone and she fetched her husband. Christy came to the telephone breathing gustily and obviously annoyed at being rung up at that hour.

'What in hell's this all about, Duke?'

'There's something I think you should know,' Morton said.

'It had better be good.'

'Depends what you call good. I'm speaking from Mr Ramirez's house.'

'Holy Jesus! what are you doing there?'

'Never mind that for the moment. Ramirez has been stabbed.'

'Stabbed! Is it bad?'

'About as bad as it could be. He's dead. His wife's been shot, and so has the housekeeper and the maid.'

'You telling me there's been four killings?'

'That's it. It's a shambles.'

There was silence at the other end. Christy seemed to be chewing on this information, and probably liking the taste of it not at all. Then he said:

'Stay there. Stay right where you are. Understand?'

'I understand,' Morton said.

There was a rattle at the other end of the line as Christy set down the receiver. He hung up too.

'I don't suppose he was overjoyed to hear the news,' Devon said.

'What do you think?'

'I think he'll be in a right splutter. Do you think he'll come here himself?'

'Not him.'

But Morton was wrong. Christy arrived with a cohort of police officers and the usual specialists who attended on such occasions. Devon guessed that he had contacted higher authority in the shape of Magnus McAndrew and maybe Edgar Roylance as well. It seemed probable that he had received orders to handle this one personally and get himself out to Jorge Ramirez's house without delay. The killing of the Colombian, following so swiftly on the havoc at Salt Cove, would have sent a lot of people into a flat spin; no doubt about that.

Christy quickly left the others to get on with their work while he took Morton and Devon aside for a little talk.

'What the devil,' he demanded, 'were you two doing here?'

Morton gave the answer they had decided on between them. It was thin, but it was the best they could think up.

'We happened to be passing and noticed that the gates were open. Knowing how security-minded Mr Ramirez was, we decided to investigate. You've seen for yourself, sir, what we found.'

'Just happened to be passing, huh?' Christy said. He had lowered his vast bulk into a large armchair and was wheezing. 'What a remarkable coincidence. Wouldn't you say it was?'

'Yes, sir. But these things happen.'

Devon could see that Christy was not swallowing it; he was not that gullible. But he seemed to have come to the conclusion that no good purpose would be served by questioning the truth of the statement. False or not, it made no difference to the fact that four people had been killed, one by a knife and the others by shooting.

'Do you have any theory regarding how this happened?'

Morton said they did, and he proceeded to spell it out. Christy gave the theory some thought and admitted, somewhat reluctantly it seemed, that it appeared to be a plausible explanation.

'And these men who worked for Mr Ramirez had gone when you arrived?'

'Long gone, I'd say,' Morton said. 'Judging by the state of the bodies. But we'll know more about that when the doc gives his report.'

'There are some jewels missing, you say?'

'Yes, sir.'

Christy turned to Devon. 'There was some business at Salt Cove last night. A flying boat and a storehouse were destroyed. There was some shooting. I suppose you wouldn't know anything about that?'

'No, sir; I wouldn't.'

'I ask,' Christy said, 'because you put in a report earlier that in your opinion the store in question contained bags of cocaine which had been brought in by the plane.'

'That is so.'

'But you were not out there last night?'

'No, sir.'

'I wonder whether anyone could confirm that.'

'I don't see how it would be possible, sir. I was alone in my chalet.'

'Yes, you would be, wouldn't you? How unfortunate that you don't have anyone living with you at present.'

Christy was touching a sensitive nerve and probably knew it. He was being vindictive because of the damage he no doubt felt certain Devon had had a hand in causing. Devon felt an inclination to sink his fist in that fat paunch; but he controlled himself.

Christy finally dismissed the two officers.

'You can go home now. Those two missing men will be found and brought to justice, never fear.'

As they were driving away in Morton's car Devon said: 'Do you think he was right?'

'Right about what?'

'About finding those two bastards and bringing them to justice.'

'Who knows?'

'Will he put us on the case, would you say?'

'I don't give a damn whether he does or not,' Morton said. 'They're still on my list. How 'bout you?'

'They're on mine too,' Devon said.

In the morning they found that they were not on the case. Devon was not surprised. He felt quite sure that Christy was convinced that the affair at Salt Cove had been at least partly his work, and it would be a black mark against his name. He had still not told anyone but Morton that he knew the murder of Jessica had been ordered by the late Jorge Ramirez and carried out by the two men who were now on the run. Morton had not revealed the fact either.

Yet Devon would not have been surprised to learn that Christy was aware of it. Or at least guessed the truth. And that went for McAndrew and Roylance too. He recalled that time when he had been interviewed by those three men and Roylance had been very sharp with the other two. It had all been an act of course. Roylance had had no intention of doing anything about the cocaine racket either. But he had felt it necessary to put on a show of taking action for Devon's benefit. And Christy and McAndrew had played their parts well. He had been completely taken in by the charade at the time.

It was all a wretched business, and he regretted now that he had got mixed up in it. Too late, he saw that his actions had done no real good whatever and had caused a great deal of harm. This was what came of being a mite too zealous and exceeding one's brief.

Morton told him that a watch was being kept on departures from the airport and a description of the two wanted men had been circulated. Unfortunately, no photographs were available and Devon feared it was all too possible that they would slip through the net. He had no confidence whatever in the ability of the Arthurton police to capture the villains.

He confided his fears to Morton. 'They'll escape. They'll get clean away and then we shall never settle our business with them.'

Morton was not much more hopeful, and he made no attempt to appear so. And he was angry. He kept the anger under control, but it was there deep down, like a rat in the stomach gnawing at him. Devon was aware of this because he felt it too. He could not forget Jessica and he knew that Morton could not forget her either. They needed to kill to assuage their anger.

They were on a routine patrol. They drove down to the waterfront and left the car and went into a bar. Morton cast an eye over the clientele and said:

'Wait here. There's someone I need to have a word with.'

He moved off down the bar and spoke to a skinny little man wearing ragged cotton trousers and a dirty T-shirt. He had a bent back and greying hair that had already deserted the front of his scalp, and there was a pair of steel-rimmed glasses resting on a pitted nose. There was an oddly furtive look about him, and he had given a sudden start when Morton touched him on the shoulder. Morton drew him away from the rest of the customers and had a brief conversation with him. Then the two of them came back to where Devon was waiting.

'This is Spider,' Morton said, keeping his voice low. 'He's got something to show us. Let's go.'

They left the bar and made their way to where Morton had parked the car. On the way he confided to Devon that Spider knew just about everything that went on along the waterfront. Devon gathered from this that the little man was an informer. It was surprising that he had lived so long, but some people led charmed lives.

They got into the car, Spider hopping into the back like a rabbit going down its burrow. Morton got the Rover moving and drove it with Spider giving directions from the back. After some manoeuvring they came to a large wooden shed not far from the harbour.

'That's it,' Spider said.

Morton stopped the car and they all got out and walked to a wide door at one end of the shed. It was closed and padlocked. Morton made no attempt to hunt up someone who might have the key. He went back to the car, opened the boot and fished out a jemmy, which was the kind of tool one might have expected a criminal to carry around rather than a police officer. He inserted the curved end of the jemmy under the hasp of the catch and put his weight on the other end. The result was gratifying; the screws securing the hasp came away from the timber and the job was done.

'Oh my Gawd!' Spider said. He glanced furtively over his shoulder to see if anyone was watching. There were some waterfront drifters lounging around, but they were some distance away and showing no interest in what was going on. 'Should you done that, Mr Morton?'

Morton did not bother to answer. He was pulling the door open. He opened it just far enough for them to squeeze through and then closed it behind them.

'Come on.'

It was hot and stuffy inside the shed, and the light coming in through a couple of dirty windows was poor. There were some crates and sacks stored inside, but they were not interested in these. The one thing of interest was a large object with a sheet of black polythene draped over it.

Morton took hold of the sheet and ripped it off.

'Ah!' he said. 'Now what have we here?'

What they had was a white Mercedes-Benz car.

Chapter Nineteen

PAY-OFF

'You seen this car before, Frank?' Morton asked.

'Could have.'

'Look to you like Mr Ramirez's car?'

'Looks very like it.'

He could not say for certain that it was the car in which the moustache and the nose had collected him that evening when he had had his meeting with Ramirez. But it was certainly the right colour and the right make, and in a place like Arthurton white Mercs were surely unlikely to be very thick on the ground. To all intents and purposes they could be certain this was Ramirez's car and that the two gorillas had left it there before moving on to somewhere else.

'So,' Morton said, 'it looks like we're on the right track.'

Spider appeared to be on edge. He said: 'Can I go now, Mr Morton? You got what you was lookin' for. I done my bit.'

'True,' Morton said. He fished some paper money out of his pocket and handed it to the little man. 'Cut along now.'

Spider stowed the money away and made for the door. In a moment he had opened it a few inches and had slipped through the gap and was gone.

'So now,' Morton said, 'we know how they're trying to get away. I think we better see what shipping there is that's about ready to leave.'

They left the shed and took the car back to a convenient parking place and began the search on foot. There were few ships to choose from, and only one of them appeared to fill the bill. It was flying the Liberian flag, which was almost certainly one of convenience, and it was lying alongside one of the piers. A blue flag with a white centre had been hoisted – the Blue Peter indicating that the vessel was preparing to leave port.

'Just in time,' Devon said.

They ran on to the pier and could see immediately just how close they had been to missing the boat – literally as well as figuratively. Two seamen on board the ship were about to release the gangplank and some port workers were at the bollards ready to unloop the cables making the vessel fast to the pier. As they reached the foot of the gangplank Morton shouted to the seamen at the upper end.

'Hold it!'

They stared at him. They were bearded and deeply tanned, and they could have been Spaniards or Italians or any one of a handful of South or Central American nationalities. But they knew enough English to understand what Morton had said. They stopped untying the gangplank.

One of them said: 'What you want?'

'We're coming aboard.'

'No,' the man said. 'Too late. We leave now. No more come board.'

'We do,' Morton said. 'We're police.' He presented the evidence. 'We have the authority.'

He was already walking up the gangplank with Devon at his heels. The seamen looked nonplussed, but they made no effort to oppose the boarding. They just shrugged expressively and stood aside.

'Follow me,' Morton said. 'And keep your gun handy.'

Devon would have made a guess that this was not the first time that Morton had had occasion to board a ship of this sort. He seemed to be familiar with the layout and he found his way without guidance to the bridge. There the two of them were confronted by a furious paunchy man in dirty whites and a peaked cap. There were frayed epaulettes on his shirt with some tarnished gold braid which signified that he was the captain. He had a jowly unshaven face and eyes like pieces of coal that had been imbedded in the flesh.

'What you do here? You have no business. I have you thrown off, by God. Don't you see we are ready to sail?'

Morton answered coolly: 'No, Captain, you will not have us thrown off. We are police officers.' Again he showed the card. 'And we do have business. Very important business. We believe two passengers came on board yesterday.'

'Passengers, passengers! This is a cargo ship, a freighter. We don't take no passengers, by God.'

'So maybe they came on board without you knowing.'

'You mean stowaways? You crazy. Nobody stow away on board my ship. Never.'

'You sure of that?'

'By God, yes. Damn sure.'

'Then would you object to us making a search?'

'Damn right, I would. Don't I tell you we ready to sail?'

There were two other men on the bridge. One was standing by the wheel, ready to take the helm when the ship began to move; the other appeared to be a junior officer. There had been one other man, but Devon had seen him slip down the ladder on the other side of the wheelhouse as soon as he and Morton appeared. It might have been significant or it might not.

'I am afraid,' Morton said, 'it won't be possible for you to sail before we have made a search.'

Devon thought the captain was going to throw a fit. His face turned purple and his eyes popped. When he spoke he seemed hardly able to articulate the words, such was his anger.

'You don't got authority. By God, you don't.'

'Wrong, Captain. We got plenty authority, and you better believe it. We can keep your ship here as long as we damn well please. We can keep it as long as it takes.'

'I have you thrown off. I give the word, it's done.'

'You'd be a fool to give the word. Are you a fool, Captain? Are you?'

He made no answer to that. He just scowled.

Morton said: 'Do you want to show us round yourself or would you rather it was somebody else? One of your officers maybe. We're easy. But the sooner we start, the sooner you get your ship out of port. It's as simple as that.'

The captain was silent for a moment or two longer, but then he seemed to come to the conclusion that he was beaten. He turned to the younger officer and snarled something unintelligible at him, making a savage gesture with his hand.

The officer, who was a slightly built young man with a hunted look about him, obviously understood the order that had been given. He spoke to Morton.

'You come with me?'

They went with him, leaving the paunchy captain fuming and muttering to himself on the bridge. The young officer seemed nervous; this was evidenced in his manner and the look in his eyes. His undisguised apprehension convinced Devon that they were on the right track. He would have made a bet that the men they were seeking were somewhere on board this ship.

It was well that Morton knew what he did about such vessels; it made it less easy for their guide to mislead them. He made one or two half-hearted attempts to do so, but Morton was having none of it. He insisted on going into the captain's own cabin and those of the other officers, but there was no one in them. In one of them, however, there was a strong scent of cigar smoke, as though someone had very recently vacated it. Devon noticed it and glanced at Morton, who gave a slight nod but said nothing.

Devon remembered the man who had left the bridge in a hurry. Had he been dispatched to give a warning? Had the men who had been smoking the cigars fled to some other part of the ship? Perhaps.

He kept his fingers on the butt of his revolver. The men they were hunting would undoubtedly be armed and ready to shoot without a moment's hesitation. It would be as well to step warily.

They went through the crew's quarters in the poop. These were filthy, reeking of sweat and dirty clothing and stale tobacco smoke. But the men they sought were not there. They left the poop and peered under the canvas awnings of the lifeboats. They looked in the forecastle and found nothing but cans of paint and brushes and coils of rope and tarpaulins and a hundred other things. No men.

The young officer said: 'You see? No stowaways. No passengers. Are you satisfied now?'

He sounded hopeful. There was even a trace of mockery in his voice. Devon guessed that he was feeling cocky. He had fooled them. He had won. Now these intruders would have to leave, empty-handed.

Morton dashed any such hopes. He said harshly: 'No, we are not satisfied. Not by a long chalk.'

'But you have searched everywhere.'

'No,' Morton said. 'Not everywhere.'

'Then what—'

'There is still the engine-room.'

'But they wouldn't be down there,' the man said; perhaps a shade too quickly.

'Now look,' Morton said. 'We've searched every other place they could be hiding and drawn a blank. So what do you think that tells a suspicious old cop like me?'

'I don't know.'

'Have a guess.'

'That they never were here?'

'Wrong. It tells me somebody tipped them off that we was on the bridge and ready to start lookin'. So they took off from the cabin they was in and made tracks for a place they reckoned would be safe as houses. That's where we're goin' now, and you're goin' to lead the way. And remember this – them guys has got guns and they'll use 'em; so mind your step 'cause you'll be between them and us; and we got guns too.'

The young officer was sweating, and the hunted look had come back with a vengeance. Devon guessed he was wishing he had never chosen to go to sea to earn his living. He could not have foreseen that he would ever be caught up in a situation such as this.

'On your way,' Morton said. 'And take care.'

There was a gantry at the top of the engine-room from which they could look down on the machinery. There was a massive diesel block centrally placed, and from this the great shaft which turned the propeller ran aft on its bearings into the tunnel leading to the stern. This was motionless at present, but the engineers down there were only waiting for the signal from the bridge to set it in motion.

It occurred to Devon that the men they were hunting might have hidden themselves in the tunnel, in which case it would be necessary to go in after them, a possible task he did not relish at all. He just hoped the Colombians were hiding somewhere else.

He and Morton were carrying their guns in their hands and were searching with their eyes for two men who did not fit in with the engine-room staff, neither engineers nor greasers. But they were nowhere to be seen. If they were indeed there, they had found a spot not visible from above.

'You see,' the young officer said. 'Nobody here that hasn't a right to be. We leave now?'

'No,' Morton said. 'We go down there. You first.'

The man hesitated. Morton prodded him with his pistol.

'Move.'

He moved then. He started to descend the iron ladder leading down from the gantry. Morton turned to Devon.

'You stay here and cover me.'

He had to go down backwards. The ladder was steep and he needed one hand to steady him by the rail. There was a second gantry halfway down. He and the young officer reached it and paused. Morton signalled to Devon to join them. When he had done so they repeated the exercise on the lower ladder, Devon staying behind to cover Morton's back.

Morton and the officer were halfway down the lower ladder when the two gorillas broke cover and started shooting. They had been crouching on the other side of the diesel block and must have decided not to wait until they were discovered but to go on the offensive at once. It was the young officer who was unlucky; he gave a scream, lost his grip and fell the rest of the way to the steel deck below. The engineers were diving for cover, not wishing to be caught in the crossfire. For them self-preservation was the order of the day.

Morton had swung round on the ladder, holding on with one hand while aiming his pistol with the other. Devon got the moustache in his sights, gripping the revolver in both hands. He had only the man's head to aim at, but it was enough; he scored with the first shot and the moustache went down with a bullet between the eyes. It was unlikely he would be getting up again.

Meanwhile, the nose and Morton were having a shoot-out and bullets were ricochetting in all directions with an angry screeching sound. Yet neither man had yet scored a hit. Devon joined in to make it a three-handed match. The nose was hopping around from place to place to make a moving target of himself, not easy to draw a bead on. He would duck under cover for a moment and suddenly reappear at some other point. Devon took a couple of shots at him and missed.

Morton decided to come down off the ladder so that he would have both hands free, but the nose caught him with a bullet in the right arm. He gave a cry and dropped his pistol. It was one up to the nose.

But this success had made him too bold. He broke cover and took a shot at Devon. It was close, but not close enough. Devon got him in the chest and he went down. Morton picked up his pistol with his left hand, walked over to where the nose was lying and put a bullet in his head. Just to make sure.

It was all over. Suddenly it had become very quiet in the engine-room and men were coming out of their holes. Devon descended the bottom ladder and had a look at Morton's arm. There was blood running down and dripping from his fingers, but it could have been a lot worse. He was wearing a short-sleeved shirt and the bullet had merely grazed his forearm; it was the blood that made it look bad.

The young officer had not even been hit. A bullet must have gone close, and the shock had made him lose his grip on the ladder. Having fallen, he had stayed down; which had been the sensible thing to do. He was bruised but otherwise uninjured.

Devon tied a handkerchief round Morton's arm to check the bleeding.

'You feeling okay?'

'Sure,' Morton said. 'Might've been dead meat without you, though. Nice shooting.'

Devon remembered the moustache. 'Better check up on the other bastard.'

Revolver in hand, he moved cautiously round to the other side of the diesel, behind which the moustache had abruptly vanished, just in case the man might be still alive and dangerous. But the caution was not necessary. The moustache was lying on his back and not moving a muscle.

Looking at him, Devon reflected on how odd it was that this man and the other should have impinged on his life with such a catastrophic effect, and yet he had never known their names.

Each had been known to him merely by a single physical feature. And now he had no desire to know anything more about them. They were dead, and he and Morton had avenged the death of Jessica, the sister of one, the lover of the other. Yet he had no sense of exultation or triumph, for this would not bring the girl back; she was gone out of his life as irrevocably as these two thugs. There was some grim satisfaction but that was all. Justice had been done; but it was a wild justice and he took no pleasure in it. He felt tired, drained, sick of it all.

The engineers were talking amongst themselves in hushed voices, casting furtive glances at him and Morton, but not addressing them by any word. He rejoined Morton.

'He's dead. Let's get out of here.'

They let their guide go up the ladders ahead of them; in fact they ordered him to. He still seemed nervous, perhaps fearing retribution from the men he had misled.

Morton went next, cursing the pain in his right arm. He too had not shown any delight at a job well and truly done. So perhaps he also was afflicted by a sense of the sheer futility of it all.

The paunchy captain was still on the bridge. No doubt he had heard the shooting and had wondered who would come out of it alive. When Morton and Devon appeared with the young officer he knew the answer.

'No passengers, huh?' Morton said. 'No stowaways either? Captain, you are one damn liar.'

He tried to brazen it out. 'What are you saying? You insult

me. I know nothing of passengers or stowaways.'

'Bullshit! There's two dead men in the engine-room and they don't belong to your crew.'

'I know nothing of that. I take nobody on board. So must be they stow away without my knowledge.'

'Bullshit again! They were thugs, murderers. How much were they paying you, Captain?'

The captain turned sullen. 'I say no more. I say nothing.'

'Makes no difference,' Morton said. 'You'll have to answer a lot of questions later. But there'll be plenty time. You won't be leaving yet awhile, so you might as well tell those guys down on the pier to go away. Right now they're not needed.'

He turned to Devon. 'Okay, Frank. Let's go call the coppers.'

Chapter Twenty

HOMECOMING

Morton came with him to the airport. But he was not driving and it was not his car. His right arm was bandaged and he was sitting in the back with Devon. There were two uniformed policemen in the front, and Devon had a feeling that they were there to make sure he got on the plane to Miami. Not that he had ever had any intention of doing otherwise. He was glad to be leaving St Joseph and he had no desire ever to return.

He was leaving early; almost two months early in fact. It had apparently been decided by certain people in Arthurton that his continued secondment to the island police force was not desirable. He found this not in the least surprising.

'I'm sorry you're going, Frank,' Morton said. 'I'll miss you.'

'Is that the truth?' Devon asked.

'Sure. You've been a pain in the arse at times, but I got used to havin' you around. Family liked you too. Specially the kids.'

'I brought you plenty of trouble.'

'You didn't mean to.'

'No, I didn't mean to.'

Least of all had he meant to cause the death of Jessica. That was something he would never forget. And never cease to regret.

'I just had to interfere. And what good did it do?'

'Don't blame yourself, Frank.'

But he did blame himself, and always would.

When the plane was in the air and heading for Miami, leaving the island of St Joseph far behind, he knew that there was something he could never leave behind. The memory.

He went to Scotland Yard after leaving Heathrow even before going home to the house in Hammersmith, which he feared would be cold, empty and unwelcoming.

Not that the welcome at headquarters was notable for any degree of warmth. Indeed, it was pretty chilly. Which was not altogether unexpected.

Detective Superintendent Alfred Lee was coldly furious.

'What in God's name have you been doing down there?'

Devon could not remember doing anything in God's name, but he thought it inadvisable to say so. This sort of flippancy might not go down well with Lee in his present mood. So he answered guardedly:

'What have they told you?'

'Nothing much. Just that you've acted in a manner not to be expected of a responsible British police officer on secondment to the Arthurton force.'

'Is that all?'

'Good grief! Isn't it enough?'

'Perhaps.'

'What do you mean, perhaps? It's plain enough that you've been misbehaving in some way. Haven't you?'

'It depends, sir, on what you mean by misbehaving. All I did was what I thought to be my duty. I admit it turned out to have some unfortunate results, and I regret that. But as for misbehaving; no, sir, I can't accept that.'

'You can't accept that, eh! Well, sit down, man, and fill me in on the sordid details.' He indicated a chair with a gesture. 'And you'd better make it good, because quite frankly, you're in the soup.'

Devon sat down. He had decided that his best course was to tell the whole of it as it had occurred from the moment when he had been met at the Arthurton airport by Detective Sergeant Marmaduke Morton.

'Marmaduke!' Lee said. 'That really his name?'

'Yes, sir. Known as Duke.'

'Ah! Well, go on, go on.'

Devon went on. He told it all, while Lee stared at him in growing amazement, breaking in now and then with questions, but remaining for the most part in silent wonder. When the story was complete he sat in silence for a while, as though running the whole thing over again in his mind and trying to come to terms with it.

Then he said: 'You killed two men?'

'I'm not sure,' Devon said. 'Morton finished one of them off, though he may have been dead already.'

'How about the men in the Catalina? Did they die?'

'Seems likely. Can't be absolutely certain, but I'd say so.'

'You seem very cool about it.'

'I'm certainly not shedding any tears over them. They were scum. Drug runners.'

Lee gave a shake of the head. 'You shouldn't have interfered. That wasn't what you were sent out there to do. It was intended to be rather in the way of a goodwill visit. Yet you seem to have taken it upon yourself to be some sort of crusader. Why?'

'I don't know. It just seemed to be the right thing. Don't you see, sir, there was this massive cocaine smuggling going on. The island had become a kind of warehouse for the Colombian suppliers. They flew the stuff in and it was shipped out to various destinations. It was one hell of a racket.'

'But it was none of your business. Don't you see? St Joseph is a poor island with few natural resources. That cocaine trade, which for the present you and this crazy American seem to have ruined, was essential to the economy. It's probable that the whole of the population will suffer for what you've done. Can't you understand that?'

'Yes, I can. But there's another side to it. The trade is immoral. It's helping to spread that poison. It's profiting by the misery of others. It ought to be stopped.'

'And you think you've stopped it?' Lee was sneering. 'You with your Boy Scout operation.'

'Of course not. But I've done what I could.'

'And a fat lot of good it's been. Do you really believe that by your efforts you'll have taken a single junkie out of circulation? A single one of them off the streets of London or Amsterdam. Don't kid yourself. If they don't get the stuff from one source they'll get it from another. The whole damn thing is out of hand.'

Devon was silent. What Lee had said was of course no less than the truth. He had sacrificed Jessica for nothing, a dream, a chimera. He had accomplished nothing.

Lee said: 'I begin to wonder, sergeant, whether you are really suited to the job of a police officer. Whether some other occupation might be more in your line.'

'I've been thinking about that myself, sir,' Devon said. And he had, all the way back from St Joseph. By the time the airliner from Miami had touched down at Heathrow he had reached a decision. 'I've come to the conclusion that it's time I did make the change.'

Lee seemed rather taken aback. 'You have?'

'Yes, sir. I'll write a formal notice of resignation and let you have it tomorrow. May I go now?'

'Yes,' Lee said, 'you may go.'

He went. And all the way down the stairs and out at the door he was asking himself the question: 'Have I been a fool? Have I been a right bloody idiot?'

And he could not be sure of the answer.

He let himself into the house. He had kept his own key with him on his travels, and it was just as well, because there was no one at home.

He had wondered whether she would be there. He had not really expected her to be. Yet he felt a touch of disappointment to discover that she was not. This feeling surprised him a little.

He dumped his luggage and went into the kitchen and made a cup of coffee. He was still drinking it when he heard the front door bang shut. He went into the hall and there she was, hanging up her raincoat.

'Chris!' he said.

She turned, and he could tell that it was quite a shock to her to see him.

'Frank!'

He had forgotten just how beautiful she was. So short a time away and he had forgotten. Seeing her now after that absence, he felt his heart leap with a kind of joy. Just like the old days.

'Yes, me,' he said.

She stared at him; and he could not tell from her expression whether she was glad or sorry to see him.

'But what are you doing here?' she said. 'I thought you were not due back for another two months.'

'I wasn't. But plans got changed.'

'Oh, I see.'

But of course she didn't.

'I didn't expect you'd still be here,' he said.

She gave a little frown of puzzlement. 'But where else would I be?'

'I seem to remember before I left there was something about your leaving me.'

'Oh, that,' she said. Dismissing it.

'I sent you a card. You didn't reply to it.'

'How could I? You didn't give me an address.'

'I rang you and got no answer.'

'I was probably out. Did you try again?'

'Yes.'

'How many times?'

'I don't remember.'

But he did. It had been just once. After that his mind had been engaged on other matters.

'Where have you been?' he asked.

'To the clinic.'

'The clinic! What clinic? There's nothing wrong, is there?'

'No,' she said. 'They tell me everything is going fine.'

'I don't understand.'

'Don't you?' she said. And laughed. 'It's very simple. I'm going to have a baby.'

He was stunned for a moment. Then he grabbed her and kissed her. And again it was just like the old days. The good old days. And maybe even better.

It had been a great homecoming after all.

Later he said: 'What shall we call her?'

'It may not be a girl.'

'It's got to be. I won't settle for anything else. A girl just like you.'

'I want a boy,' she said.

'Are we going to fight over this?'

'No,' she said. 'No more fights. Ever. Right?'

'Right.'

'I love you, Frank. I'm glad you came back early. It's been so lonely without you.'

'I love you too, Chris.'

'What was it like in St Joseph?'

'It was just like you said. Some job.'

'Going to tell me about it?'

'Some other time, Chris, some other time.'

And even then not the whole of it. No, certainly not the whole of it. Ever.

'I'd better tell you,' he said. 'I've quit my job.'

She stared. 'You don't mean it.'

'I do.'

'You mean you won't be a policeman any more?'

'That's it.'

'But what will you do?'

'I'll find something.'

He had to. He would soon have a family to support.

One day a picture postcard arrived from Jamaica. It had been addressed to him at Scotland Yard, London, and had been sent on from there. There was a photograph of Montego Bay and a brief message which read:

'Having a great time. Hoping you are well. Regards. Adam.'

He showed it to Christine.

'Who's Adam?' she asked.

'A man I used to know once upon a time.'

'A friend of yours?'

He thought about that for a while. Then he said: 'No, I don't think so. Not really. In fact I think it would have been better if I had never met him.'